Someplace Else

by Ben Shecter

HARPER & ROW, PUBLISHERS

New York, Evanston, San Francisco, London

SOMEPLACE ELSE   Copyright © 1971 by Ben Shecter

Library of Congress Catalog Card Number: 77-146003

Trade Standard Book Number—06-025576-5
Harpercrest Standard Book Number—06-025577-3

First Edition

FOR CHARLOTTE

Chapters

Someplace Else

1. Someplace New

What would happen if I rubbed the hunchback's hump? Arnie thought. It's supposed to bring good luck. He wondered if it was true, and if it was, how you go about doing it. Do you just ask? Or do you slap him on the back and say, "How're ya doin', old pal?" Or maybe when he's bending down, sneak in a rub. He watched the dwarf-like beggar with the yellow dog go from one garbage pail to another.

Everything was different in the new neighborhood. There weren't any trees on the streets, and the houses were old brown brick, and squeezed together. Arnie was waiting for his father to come home from work, and today he was late.

The old house and yard seemed a long time ago. Arnie knew his father didn't want to sell the store and take a factory job. He remembered the day he found out they were going to move. "Circumstances force us to make a change," his mother said. And his father said, "It's just a temporary thing."

After that, the house Arnie had known all his life began to change. Familiar things disappeared into boxes, and he had to give his rabbit away. "An apartment's no place for a rabbit!" said his mother. When Arnie couldn't hide his tears, his mother said, "Crying over a rabbit—is that any way for a boy of eleven to act?"

It was a summer of packing and unpacking, and listening to his mother complain about the Oriental rug being too big for the new apartment. With the move, talk of Arnie's bar mitzvah began, and of finding a good rabbi for him. Arnie just wanted to be left alone to work on his magic cabinet. He had wanted to be a magician from the time his father took him to see a stage show with a really terrific magic act. Now, work at the factory prevented those Saturday outings, and Arnie missed them —he really liked being with his father.

These days Arnie felt like a visitor in the apartment. There didn't seem to be any room, or time, for him or his magic.

He looked down the street, hoping to see his

father. But he was nowhere in sight. The beggar had made a raincoat for his dog out of paper and string, and now he was looking at Arnie—who felt uncomfortable and looked up at the sky, pretending he didn't notice. The sky was filled with thick mud-colored clouds that began to grumble. A group of boys ran down the street shouting and kicking at a box until it broke and splintered.

"You'd better stay away from them; they're pretty mean."

Arnie looked up and saw a fat girl with eyeglasses standing in the doorway.

"I'm Gloria Becker," she said. "We're neighbors; we live in 2C."

Arnie said hello, although he didn't want to.

"You're the Schiffman boy. I saw your name on the mailbox."

Arnie nodded. Little Miss Detective, he thought. Not wanting to encourage any more talk, Arnie turned away and looked down the street for his father.

"We'll be going to the same school," she said. "See you soon."

Not if I can help it, Arnie said to himself.

Raindrops had begun to fall. Arnie's father

ran down the street with a newspaper over his head and a package under his arm. "Just in time," his father laughed. Arnie was happy to see his father. He had a way of making things seem all right. His father handed him the package. "Something for you," he said. Arnie tore open the box. Inside was a trick rubber chicken.

"For my production cabinet!" he shouted. Arnie held the rubber chicken by the legs and raced his father up the stairs.

2.   Good-bye, Fiona

Arnie balanced the laundry basket on his head while he waited impatiently for the washing machine to stop. Doing the laundry in the basement was a new chore that Arnie really hated. He told his mother it was girls' work. He also wanted to avoid being seen by "Barnacle Becker," a name he had given to Gloria. She had become buddy-buddy with his mother, and a real pain for him.

"Have you seen a white mouse?" asked the boy who had come up quietly behind Arnie.

The basket fell and Arnie shook his head no.

The boy continued speaking, "She's not in the garbage—I just went through it."

Arnie was unhappy about being seen with the wash, even though the pimply-faced boy looked like the kind everyone chased and called sissy.

"You new here?" asked the boy.

Arnie shook his head yes.

"I'm Elliot Gold," he said, fingering a big pimple on his chin.

"I'm Arnie Schiffman." The washing machine stopped and Arnie began to empty it. "Live here a long time?" asked Arnie, wondering if the pimple had broken, and it was safe to turn around.

"Oh, we don't live in this building," said Elliot. "We live across the street. My mother just comes here to do the wash and throw my mice away." Elliot got on his knees and looked for his mouse. "Last time, I found her in the washing machine."

Arnie searched through his basket of wash. "It's not in here."

"It's a good thing," said Elliot. "She would have been one very clean, but very dead mouse."

Arnie spotted the mouse sipping water from a hose. "There she is!" he said, pointing.

Elliot quickly caught the mouse and kissed her. "Thanks. My mother hates her, but Fiona's no ordinary mouse."

"I don't imagine she is, with a name like Fiona," said Arnie, petting the mouse. Elliot gave Arnie the mouse to hold. "What's so special about her?" asked Arnie.

Before Elliot had a chance to answer they

were interrupted by Gloria, who was looking for Arnie. "Arnold, your mother was wondering what happened to you!"

"I got stuck in the washing machine," said Arnie.

"Elliot Gold," she said, making his name sound like a disease, "are you still playing around with those disgusting mice?"

"You mean this?" said Arnie holding the mouse right in front of Gloria's face, and she ran screaming from the basement. Arnie and Elliot had a good laugh. "She's the original pain," said Arnie, and Elliot agreed with him. Arnie handed the mouse back to him.

"Fiona knows how to go through a maze I built," Elliot said. "I'm going to be a scientist."

Arnie told Elliot about the rabbit he once had, and then he lied. He told Elliot that he had a complete magic act, and that he performed in shows. Arnie remembered what his father had told him about a person being liked for what he is, and not what he pretends to be. He felt ashamed when Elliot said, "I never knew anyone with an act before."

Elliot asked Arnie if he wanted to see his

chemistry set. "Sure!" said Arnie, "But it will have to be some other time. My father is taking me to see a rabbi about bar mitzvah lessons."

"I'm getting bar mitzvahed soon," said Elliot. "Whatever you do, don't go to Rabbi Bliesch. He's a loser."

That night after dinner Arnie went with his father to a rabbi.

Why would anyone paint a room such a rotten color, Arnie thought, looking at the faded mustard ceiling of the rabbi's study. He thought about all the great colors he could choose from when it was time to paint his magic cabinet.

"This is my Kaddishel," said Arnie's father proudly to the rabbi. The waxen-looking man with the stained beard smiled at Arnie. His father had told him bar mitzvah was a happy time. How could any happiness come from this rabbi, he wondered.

The rabbi stood slightly bent with a yellowing prayer shawl covering him, and he spoke as if he was trying to hold back a good cry. His musty-smelling room was piled high with books. They spilled out from the walls onto the chairs, tables, and even the floor. Arnie found himself wishing he weren't Jewish. He tried to push the thought away, but it was locked in. Arnie couldn't help but feel that if God knew what he was thinking He'd punish him, especially here at the rabbi's. Would He make him like the hunchbacked beggar? Or would God see to it that he never practiced another magic trick again? Arnie thought about miracles. If he had God's power, he could become the most famous magician in the world.

The rabbi looked at Arnie. "When you are thirteen you'll have your bar mitzvah, the old Jewish custom celebrating the reaching of manhood." The rabbi rocked gently back and forth as he spoke. Arnie was sure he could celebrate his manhood with a private little party and easily forget all about ancient customs. Arnie felt left out, as his father and the rabbi spoke to each other in Yiddish. He hated it when his father spoke Yiddish; he felt as if his father didn't belong to him.

An old clock hiding among the books chimed, and as if it were a signal the rabbi's thin blue-veined hand appeared from beneath his shawl.

"Thank you, Rabbi Bliesch," said his father, shaking the rabbi's hand. The rabbi sneezed, and Arnie wondered if he should say "God bless you." He didn't say anything; he remained silent until they were out of the house.

"Did you smell his breath? I think he's been gargling with garbage." Arnie laughed at his own joke. "And what about that crazy thing he was wrapped in—he must think he's Sitting Bull!"

His father looked at him disapprovingly and told him not to judge people by what they wear, or by the smell of their breath. "There are better ways to judge people," he said.

Arnie walked a few steps behind his father, his chin buried in his chest and hands deep into his pockets. He was miserable. Rabbi Bliesch might be the greatest guy in the whole world, Arnie thought, but he didn't want to see him every day after school for two years.

"Dad, what does Kaddishel mean?" Arnie asked.

"It means that when I die you will say the Mourner's Prayer for me as I did for my father."

Arnie walked the rest of the way home alongside his father.

3. Banana Cake

The Sunday morning quiet was broken by Arnie's mother. "Put on your good pants today," she said. "We are going to Bubba's." Arnie called his grandmother Bubba. She was his mother's mother.

"She'll be happy to know we found a rabbi for your bar mitzvah lessons," said his father.

Visits to Bubba meant banana cake, halvah, and homemade jam on pumpernickel bread. Going to Bubba's also meant visiting with Aunt Fran, Uncle Henry, and cousins Susan and Amy. They all lived together in a big house. Bubba lived downstairs; Aunt Fran and Uncle Henry lived upstairs. There, Arnie would play Monopoly with his cousins. Sometimes Susan who was older would let him use her typewriter, and he would make up stories. In the summer, honeysuckle vines touched the roof of their house, and it was hard to see in or out of the windows.

Inside Bubba's apartment it was dark and

cool and the furniture smelled of lemon. Bubba was old. Once when her white hair wasn't combed into a bun, Arnie saw that it was long and it fell way down her back. He thought she looked like some kind of witch.

Bubba told him many stories about the old country. And she knew things like how it was bad luck to open an umbrella indoors, and if a black cat crosses your path, spit. It was from her that he learned about rubbing a hunchback's hump for good luck. Arnie entertained Bubba with his magic, and when he'd always guess the card she picked, she'd spit and say he was possessed by a dybbuk. He asked his father what a dybbuk was. He told him it was a spirit that moves into someone's body rent-free. Arnie liked the idea of there being a secret spirit inside of him. He pretended that this spirit belonged to an ancient magician. He even named the spirit Amir.

When Arnie's mother spoke about the new apartment, his grandmother asked her if she had remembered to put salt and bread in a cabinet. When his mother said she'd forgotten, Bubba put her hands to her head and cried, "It shouldn't be too late!" Then she ran

and gave his mother a box of salt and a slice of bread.

"What's that for?" asked Arnie.

"It's salt to keep the devil away, and bread to make sure your house is never in need of food," said his grandmother.

When it was time to leave Arnie kissed his grandmother and said, "Bubba, you make the best banana cake in the whole world."

"Just for that," she said, "I'm going to give you a whole cake to take home."

4. Elliot's Experiment

Soon after his visit to Bubba's, Arnie sat in front of the building twisting the rubber chicken's neck. He had just begun to work on his magic cabinet when his mother told him he had to get out of the apartment. "You can't stay here when I use roach killer," she said.

Elliot Gold, looking unhappy, came by and sat down. He stroked the fuzz above his lip as if it were a mustache.

"How's Fiona?" asked Arnie.

"I don't know. She got out of her cage this morning, and now my mother has a trap set up."

Elliot and Arnie sat silently, each sinking deeper into his own gloom. Finally Elliot broke the silence with a deep sigh. "Well, we could always make stink bombs!" he said.

"Stink bombs?"

"Yeh, it's a mixture that smells like rotten eggs."

Arnie laughed. "Boy, that really must smell!"

"Come on. I'll make one now."

Arnie followed Elliot into his apartment. "Where's your mother?" whispered Arnie.

"She works at the grocery store, with my father."

"My father used to have a store," said Arnie. "And as soon as this temporary thing is over, we're going to get another one." Elliot's room looked like a chemical warehouse. Every inch of space was taken up with things in bottles, glass test tubes, and pipes of many sizes and shapes. "You sure got a lot of stuff."

"I've got my own Bunsen burner," said Elliot. "Do you want me to cook your chicken on it?"

"No, thanks, I'm going to have supper soon," laughed Arnie.

"What's it for, anyway?" asked Elliot, who began to mix things from little bottles into a glass beaker.

"It's for my magic production cabinet," said Arnie, "if I ever get a chance to finish it." He looked at Elliot but Elliot didn't seem to remember his lie about having an act.

16

"Okay, what's a magic production cabinet?"

"It's really a great piece of magical equipment. At first, I show the audience this beautiful cabinet with nothing in it. Then, with a few magic words I can take all sorts of stuff out of it, like this chicken."

"Sounds terrific," said Elliot, who was holding the glass beaker over the flame with a pair of tongs. Arnie watched the beaker, expecting some magic trick to happen. "I once brought one of these stink bombs to Hebrew school. Boy, did I clear the place out!" Elliot laughed, pleased by the memory. The mixture over the flame began to bubble. "Do you want a cigarette?" he asked, bending down to light one at the Bunsen burner. "Yikes!" he yelled, as he singed the fuzz above his lip and dropped the mixture to the floor. The glass beaker broke and the room began to fill with yellow smoke.

Arnie held his nose. "It's beginning to stink in here!"

Elliot opened the windows wide. "Let's go to the roof till it clears," he said.

From the rooftop, the neighborhood looked different. A feeling of excitement touched Arnie. "You can see everything from up here!"

He went from one part of the roof to another.

Elliot watched a flock of pigeons circling around. "Did you ever want to run away?" he asked. Arnie avoided the question and began to ask about different buildings. Elliot answered like a guide on a touring bus. He spoke out of the side of his mouth. "—And over there is the river, and if you look real hard you can see the bridge and the Wilcox house near it. Some people say it's haunted."

"Really haunted!" exclaimed Arnie, who liked the idea of ghosts and supernatural things.

"I heard about this guy who went there and—" Elliot's voice trailed off and he put his hand to his ear.

"What's the matter?" asked Arnie.

"Listen—do you hear anything?"

Arnie listened. "Fire engines!"

"Oh, oh, not again!" moaned Elliot. They watched the fire trucks pull up in front of the building. Huddled near the roof door, they could hear the firemen speaking in the hallway. "It's that crazy kid and his chemistry set again," they said.

After the fire trucks had gone, they waited a

bit longer and then left the roof. Arnie retrieved his chicken and went home. "Have a busy day, Arnold?" asked Gloria, who was sitting in front of the building knitting.

5. Hate Day

Arnie's father fidgeted with his new eyeglasses as he read the newspaper. Since he'd been working at the factory he often complained about his eyes. "It's tedious work," he told Arnie, "polishing lenses all day."

Arnie lay stretched out on the floor near him reading the comics. "Hate day is almost here," he mumbled.

His father looked up from the paper. "What did you say?"

"Hate day is almost here," said Arnie.

"What's hate day?" asked his father.

"You know, there's Flag Day, and Arbor Day, and days like that. Well, the first day of school is hate day."

"Why don't you write a letter to the President and he can make it a national holiday, and all the schools will be closed on hate day," said his father.

"But then there'd be two hate days, because the next day you'd have to go to school anyway," Arnie said, going back to the comics. His father smiled.

Hate day arrived, and Arnie walked to school with a rotten feeling in his stomach. The classroom had a kind of old library-paste smell from being closed all summer. After weeks of polo shirts and dungarees, Arnie felt warm and uncomfortable in his starched white shirt, and tie. "You've got to make a good impression," his mother had said.

Arnie wished he could pull the greatest disappearing act of all time. He felt as if he didn't belong—all the kids knew each other from the year before. The teacher, Miss Noonan, wasn't young and pretty like Miss Robbins at his old school. She seemed cranky and impatient as she gave orders, and she was always patting her hair into place. She seated the class according to height, except for those who wore glasses. Arnie sat in back of the room because he was third tallest in line. Miss Noonan quickly got to the business of appointing monitors, most of whom were girls. She made a speech about this being an important time for them because next year they would be going on to Junior High. She also told them about how she was in charge of the major dramatic production for the entire school, and how her past projects were noted for their excellence. Arnie figured she must have been doing it for at least a hundred and ten years. She ended her speech with, "Remember you'll have to work hard to qualify for graduation." Arnie wanted to be back at the other school where he could graduate with all the kids he knew.

The tallest boy in the class, who sat to the right of Arnie, tossed him a note. Arnie opened the wrinkled piece of paper and read it: NERVOUS NOONAN HAS NO HAIR. SHE WEARS A WIG.

Miss Noonan yelled, "Give me that note!"

Arnie slipped the note into his pocket. She slammed a book closed and walked directly to Arnie. Close up, he was able to see that her rust-colored hair didn't seem to be growing from her head, and her eyebrows were only pencil-thin lines.

"Who tossed you that note and where is it?" she demanded.

It was at times like this that Arnie wished Amir the magician could turn someone like her into a tadpole. Or else he wished his father were there to tell her to stop picking on him.

"Where is that note?" she asked again.

Arnie was scared. "I don't have any note," he said, opening his hands. Then she looked at Arnie for a very long time. He got a funny feeling, like he had to go to the bathroom. All the kids looked at him, and some of the girls covered their mouths and giggled.

After lunch he walked slowly back to school. He wished he was all grown up so he wouldn't have to go to Hebrew school and public school —he just wanted to be by himself. He wondered, with the way his luck was going, how he had avoided running into Gloria.

Then Arnie heard someone calling him. It was the boy who tossed the note. He smiled, and from his appearance Arnie knew he was the kind of guy everyone wanted for his best friend.

"Hey, I'm sorry," he said. "Thanks for not squealing."

"That's okay," said Arnie. "I hate her anyway."

"That makes two of us." They shook hands in agreement. "My name is Harvey Bloom. I'm the tallest guy in the class. I'll probably be captain of the basketball team. I was last year. Do you play basketball?"

"Sure!" said Arnie. But he was lying—he was a rotten basketball player.

"We practice in the gym after school."

Arnie felt relieved. "That leaves me out. I've got bar mitzvah lessons after school."

"That's tough. See ya," he said running off to join a group of boys. Arnie wished he knew how to play basketball.

The afternoon was spent distributing books and carrying in supplies. Miss Noonan had most of the kids help her, but she didn't ask Arnie. She walked to the back of the room several times, and once she stopped to ask him about the note. When the bell sounded and it was time to leave, Miss Noonan told him to stay. The first day of school always seemed like the longest day of the year and Arnie knew this was going to be a record-breaker. He also wondered what his mother was going to say about the ink he'd gotten on his shirt.

Miss Noonan put on gardening gloves and searched her plants for bugs. "Little devil!" she'd squeal every time she scrunched one to death. When she was finished she told Arnie he could leave. "We're not off to a good start," she said, putting on her hat and thrusting a

large pin through it. At that moment Arnie
hoped her aim was bad.

When his father got home from work he
asked Arnie how hate day was.

"Long," said Arnie. "Very long."

"I know," his father said.

Arnie looked at his father's face. He does
know, Arnie thought.

6. Finders Keepers

Slate-colored bands stretched across the sky. The days were getting shorter. A cool wind made Arnie shiver and wish he'd worn a warmer sweater, like his mother had told him to. He walked home from Hebrew school on what had now become a familiar route.

Rabbi Bliesch was the loser Elliot Gold had said he was, and Arnie's first impression of Miss Noonan stuck. The Oriental rug was rolled and hidden behind the sofa, and Arnie's magic cabinet was still unfinished. His mother complained about being tired, and when his father came home from work he spoke about shop chairmen, and foremen, and company policy. He'd often tell Arnie how important it was to be his own boss when he grew up. The situation that was going to be a temporary thing began to settle, like a toy left out in the yard all year.

As Arnie passed the vacant lot he spied a

little dog wandering in the rubble. It was hard for him to pass an animal without petting or talking to it. He followed the scrawny white puppy across the garbage-strewn lot.

Big John Mackie, who everyone called Crazy John because he was retarded, watched Arnie and yelled, "You'll never get 'im, never get 'im!" Arnie played a game about people who belonged together in a family. In this family, Big John was related to the hunch-backed beggar and Miss Noonan.

"Here, pup! Here, pup!" Arnie called, stumbling through bedsprings and old shoes.

"You'll never get 'im, never get 'im!" said Big John over and over again.

The pup sprawled out on a moldy cushion, and looked up at Arnie. "Hey pup, don't be afraid, it's only me," said Arnie kneeling down to pet him. He noticed that the dog had one blue eye and one brown. Big John walked over to them. Arnie was afraid of John Mackie, because he was big and strong, and unpredictable.

"He don't belong to no one," said Big John. "I gave him spaghetti the other day."

"You sure are skinny." Arnie could feel the puppy's bones under his short matted hair. He picked him up. "Whew, you smell bad! What you need is a bath, and some real food."

"He's real dirty, isn't he," said Big John.

"He sure is!" said Arnie, feeling his fingers getting sticky as he continued petting the dog.

"Let's give 'im a bath," said Big John, trying to take the pup out of Arnie's arms.

Arnie was frightened and he held the dog tightly. "No, it's all right, John—I—I think I know who he belongs to," said Arnie pulling away from Big John. "I'll see you." Big John watched Arnie walk, then run, down the street and disappear around a corner.

The puppy licked Arnie's ear. "Hey, that tickles," laughed Arnie. While holding the puppy, he thought of his rabbit and wondered how he was. "I once had a rabbit," Arnie told the puppy, who began to lick Arnie's chin. "Hey, cut it out!" But he really liked having the pup licking him—it felt good.

Afraid to go upstairs with the puppy, he sat in front of the building wondering what to do. "My mother said I can't have any pets in the apartment, but you really are something special—I mean, not every dog has one blue eye and one brown."

"Hey, Arnie, whatcha got there?" Elliot shouted from his window.

"A puppy," said Arnie holding the dog up.

"Can you keep it?" asked Elliot.

"I think so," said Arnie. "We can try," he whispered to the pup.

"Absolutely not! You can't keep him," said Arnie's mother.

"But he's probably worth a lot of money," said Arnie, trying to appeal to the practical side of his mother. "He's a very unusual dog— did you look at his eyes?"

Arnie's mother looked at the puppy. "He's probably sick and diseased!"

For as long as Arnie could remember, whenever his mother didn't want him to have something, she said it was diseased or the people who touched it were. Like the time he wanted the hamburger from the old vendor at the beach.

"Can't we just give him a little something to eat?" pleaded Arnie.

His mother hesitated a moment. "Well, just give him some of those leftover meatballs, and then he's got to go."

The puppy gulped the meatballs down. "Boy, is he hungry!" said Arnie.

"Here give him some of this," she said, handing Arnie some chicken scraps. "Take the bones out!" she warned. "I heard somewhere that chicken bones are bad for dogs."

The puppy ate the chicken and stretched out near the stove. "The poor pup has probably been cold and starving for days." Arnie tried hard to arouse his mother's sympathy.

"That's what happens when you're born into the world with no one to care for you," said his mother.

"It's kind of terrible," said Arnie, who found himself praying to God and making all sorts of promises if his mother would break down and let him keep the pup.

"Do you ever stop to think about all the poor homeless children?"

"All the time," said Arnie, who couldn't have cared less about homeless children.

Gloria walked in, loaded down with magazines. Arnie sighed unhappily; he didn't want to have to beg for the dog in front of Gloria.

"My mother thought you might want to see these," she said, putting the magazines down on the kitchen table.

"Thank you, dear," said Arnie's mother, stepping over the pup, as she checked the food on the stove.

"What's that?" asked Gloria, pointing to the pup.

"An elephant," said Arnie.

Mrs. Schiffman turned to Arnie and shook a mixing spoon at him. "Don't be smart," she said. It made Arnie feel good to see the puppy sleeping by the warm stove.

"He looks very dirty," said Gloria. "Do you think he has germs?"

"He needs a good scrubbing," said his mother.

"Can't I just have him for a few days?" pleaded Arnie. Arnie found himself begging with Gloria there, but he didn't care, he wanted the puppy.

"My mother says dogs are a lot of work," said Gloria.

"She should know, if she raised you," Arnie mumbled. The little dog yawned and whimpered. "Dogs are great pets," said Arnie, almost trying to convince Gloria as well as his mother. Arnie's mother looked at the puppy for a long time, the pup looked back at her almost pleadingly.

33

"What's going to happen when he makes all over the house?"

"He won't. I'll take good care of him— you'll see." Arnie ran and picked up the puppy. "I'll walk him twenty times a day. I promise."

"Your father will think I've lost my mind, but we'll give it a try."

Arnie hugged the puppy. "You're mine!" he whispered. "You're mine!"

"You can throw the magazines out when you're through with them," said Gloria. "But then again, you might want to keep them for when he does mess."

7. The Bird's Nest

For one whole week, Mrs. Schiffman spoke about nothing else but getting to the cemetery before the cold weather started. Arnie had never known his father's parents or his mother's father. They had died before he was born. To Arnie, they were just people in photographs.

Always before, he had to stay home when his parents visited the cemetery, but now that he was preparing for his bar mitzvah, his father said he was old enough to go. Arnie didn't want to go, he wanted to stay with his dog.

He had named the puppy Houdini after the famous magician, because he thought there was something magical about a dog with two different colored eyes. "I don't want to go to the cemetery," Arnie said, patting Houdini.

His parents insisted. "It's like going to the country," said his mother.

In order to get an early start, breakfast was postponed. Buttered rolls and a thermos of hot coffee were packed for the trip. The car had been sold, so it meant taking two buses to get there. The second bus went directly to the cemetery. Arnie sat next to a window and watched the people get on the bus. "All aboard the cemetery express!" he said, loud enough for some people to turn around and look. His mother, sitting behind him, tapped him on the head. His father was silent during the trip. There was a faraway look in his eyes—he seemed sad. It was an expression Arnie was beginning to see more often, and he hated to see his father look like that.

Brown and yellow leaves blew across the cemetery. An old bearded man who read the prayer at the grave approached them. Arnie followed his mother and father until they came to a big gray gravestone with the name Schiff-man on it, and he read the names—Bella Schiffman and Arnold W. Schiffman. Arnie had been named after his grandfather even to the middle W., which stood for Warren. He knew right then that his name would look just like that on a gravestone in this or another cemetery. He thought of the bird he had once buried in his backyard, and how, when he dug

it up some time later, it was just a mess, with little white bugs eating at it.

He whispered softly, "I'm never going to die, never going to die—" He said it over and over again like a chant, hoping that when he finished it would be true.

He ate a buttered roll while the old man in black said a prayer. A bird's nest blew onto a grave. Arnie picked it up.

"What are you going to do with that?" his mother asked.

"I'm going to take it home," said Arnie.

"Leave it here," said his mother. "It's bad luck to take anything home from a cemetery."

Arnie hid the nest under his jacket.

8. Bar Mitzvah

It was Elliot's bar mitzvah day. "Are you scared?" Arnie asked him. Elliot just shrugged his shoulders in reply. Arnie looked at Elliot as if he had never seen him before. He looked different with his hair slicked down, and dressed in a new overcoat. "You sure are lucky," said Arnie. "I wish mine was over with."

"Well, mine isn't over yet," said Elliot, with an edge to his voice. "I'll see ya. I gotta be there before everyone else." Elliot turned and walked away.

"Do you want me to walk you?" Arnie called after him. Replying again with the shrug of his shoulders, Elliot continued walking ahead. Catching up, Arnie walked alongside him. They walked for a while without saying a word to each other—the only sound came from Elliot's new shoes squeaking.

"Are a lot of people coming?" asked Arnie, trying to break what seemed like an uncomfortable silence. Elliot remained silent. Arnie was beginning to regret walking with him. He felt that Elliot was quickly becoming a stranger, partly because of Elliot's funny way of acting and partly because Arnie felt that Elliot was going on to other things, leaving him behind.

"I guess things will be different now," said Arnie.

"Why?" asked Elliot.

"Well, you getting to be a man and everything."

"I don't feel different."

"You're acting different," said Arnie.

"Well, so are you," said Elliot, looking directly at him.

"I am?" said Arnie, surprised.

"Yeh, and you aren't even getting bar mitzvahed." Elliot sighed and then made a confession. "I'm so nervous I threw up my breakfast."

Wanting to make Elliot feel better, Arnie thought of good things to say. "You sure look sharp," he said. "Even your face has cleared up."

"Thanks—but this tie is strangling me." Elliot spoke in a choking voice.

"Just think about the party after services, and the presents you'll get."

"Don't remind me of the party," Elliot said with a gloomy expression. "That's all I've heard from my mother for weeks. You'd think *she* was getting bar mitzvahed. Do you know— I couldn't sit in the living room for the last two days because my mother said I'd mess it up for the party." Almost on the verge of tears, Elliot's voice softened to a whisper. "Not only that, but she vacuumed up Fiona, dead."

Arnie put his arm on Elliot's shoulder. "That's rotten," he said. "Well, at least there won't be any more Rabbi Bliesch." And that made Elliot smile.

The synagogue was filled with its regular Saturday morning worshippers, as well as the friends and family of Elliot Gold. It was easy to tell them apart. Most of the Saturday regulars were old and quiet—the guests were younger, more dressed up, and noisier. Arnie sat in a back pew.

In keeping with an old custom, the shamus handed out bags of candy to the children so that they could throw it at Elliot after services. The shamus, who was like the manager of the synagogue, was an irritable old man who always used to yell at all the Hebrew school boys for stuffing the toilets with candy wrappers. He once threatened to make Arnie clean the bowl after he discovered a big wad of bubble gum floating around. The shamus was also a big phony, guilty of one of the worst crimes any grown-up could commit—when the parents were around, he would always act over-nice.

The shamus passed up Arnie when he was distributing bags of candy, and whether it was done on purpose or not, Arnie was just as happy. "I don't want anyone boffing me on the head with candy bags," Arnie said to himself.

Elliot and his father stood at the altar with Rabbi Bliesch, who had changed suits for the occasion. Instead of the old shiny gray one he wore all the time, he wore an old shiny black one.

Elliot chanted his part of the service in an uneven, cracking, changing voice. Feeling uncomfortable and embarrassed for Elliot, Arnie felt like slipping off of the bench and crawling out of the synagogue. It was almost the same feeling Arnie got when Miss Noonan sang

"The Star Spangled Banner" in her crazy, false soprano voice. The thing that made Arnie especially uncomfortable about Elliot's performance was the fact that he was a friend.

After all the bags of candy had been thrown, everyone went back to Elliot's house for the party. The small apartment was crowded with people, and there wasn't a trace of any chemistry equipment in Elliot's room. In its place were folding tables covered over with fancy paper tablecloths and piles of food.

"But it's my bar mitzvah!" pleaded Elliot.

"Never mind. You'll do as I say," said his mother. "When you eat, you'll put a napkin in your collar. But before you eat, go get some cream soda from the fire escape."

"Hey, let's get out of here," said Elliot, who found Arnie standing quietly in a corner. They grabbed some sandwiches and left. They ate them when they were sitting near the narrow canal that ran in back of the silk mill.

"This sure beats my rotten party," said Elliot. "How was I at services?"

"Oh you were great, just great!" said Arnie. Suddenly he had trouble swallowing his sandwich. He wondered if his bar mitzvah would ever happen, and how he would do.

9. Arnie's Hex

Twirling skeletons smiled down on laughing witches. Arnie looked up at the Halloween decorations and tickled a skeleton's foot.

Instead of going directly to Hebrew school, Arnie wandered through the five-and-dime. He wanted to buy a present for Houdini. Passing a counter piled high with masks, he stopped to look at a monster face, and when he thought no one was looking he put it on. Seeing his reflection in a glass case, Arnie made a grunting noise.

"Okay, Frankenstein, you either buy it, or hands off the merchandise."

Frightened, Arnie pulled the mask off, tearing the elastic band.

"I oughta make you pay for it," said the salesgirl. She wore a big button with the name Rhoda printed on it, and under her name it read, "Vote for your favorite salesgirl."

"You're not going to win, Rhoda!" said

Arnie, running out of the store. He felt unhappy about not getting anything for Houdini. He walked slowly toward Hebrew school
thinking about monsters and ghouls, and
Amir, the spirit living inside of him. He began
to imagine Amir materializing and looking
like the monster mask. "Boy, could we scare
the pants off of that dumb Rhoda," he laughed
to himself.

Arnie heard shouting behind him. It was
the tough boys Gloria had once warned him
about. They were laughing and saying dirty
things out loud. Arnie started to walk fast. He
had a feeling something bad was going to happen. He dropped a Hebrew book and didn't
turn to pick it up. Then he began to run.

Arnie ran all the way to the rabbi's, and at
the door he quickly looked around, but the
boys were nowhere in sight. He sighed. He was
hot and cold, and felt like vomiting.

"You're late again," coughed the rabbi as
he let Arnie in. "Ten minutes late!" He held
out a pocket watch on a long chain and tapped
it with a crooked finger.

Arnie had to take a deep breath before he
could speak. His mouth was dry and the

words seemed stuck inside. "I'm sorry, Rabbi Bliesch. I had some trouble and—"

"Always trouble, always excuses—maybe you'll be late for your bar mitzvah."

Arnie followed the rabbi down the long dark corridor. His clothes were damp with sweat, and he combed the wet hairs off of his forehead with his fingers. The rabbi mumbled things about respect, but Arnie only half listened to him. He thought about the tough kids and the book he had left behind. Arnie took his place on the hard wooden bench next to Willie Fiedler. "Hi, Willie," he said.

Willie Fiedler was a small pale boy who had started lessons the same time as Arnie, only he was doing much better. Willie offered Arnie some peanuts.

"Shaaa!" said the rabbi, brewing tea on a hot plate.

Willie thought Arnie was the greatest because he made good cartoons of the rabbi blowing his nose. "Draw the rabbi," whispered Willie, with a mischievous look in his eyes.

Arnie shook his head no. Willie's expression changed to one of hurt. Almost mechanically

Arnie began to draw the rabbi. While drawing he thought about the clay dolls he had made the other day. One with a cotton beard and one with red wool hair. He called the dolls Rabbi and Miss Noonan and stuck pins in them. The dolls were hidden in a shoebox marked "trading cards," along with the bird's nest and other secret things. The thought of having his mother discover what was really in the shoebox made Arnie shiver.

Arnie stopped drawing and hugged himself. It was cold inside the synagogue. A wind swept through the room and set the crystals tinkling on the lopsided chandelier above the altar.

"Rabbi, why don't you turn the radiators up?" asked Willie.

"Radiators? When I was your age we were lucky to have a roof over our heads," said the rabbi, warming his hands on a glass of tea. Seating himself on a cracked leather chair the rabbi took his place at the table, opposite the boys. He opened a bottle of smelly medicine and nodded to Willie to begin the lessons.

Willie began chanting in his high, squeaky voice. The rabbi listened with closed eyes.

Arnie fixed his eyes on the rabbi's tobacco-stained fingers, curled around the glass of tea. Then he scribbled a note. "Dear rabbi, you have dirty fingers—wear gloves." He signed it "A good friend." Shredding the note into dozens of pieces, he let it fall to the floor like snow. He looked around the room and decided that the drape-covered Torah cabinet would make a great piece of magic equipment. He thought about how terrific it would be if one day during Saturday services the rabbi would pull back the drape to get at the Torah and find a hundred birds flying out of the cabinet. Grinning, Arnie looked out of a window near the table. He closed one eye and looked through a rip in the soiled white window curtain. The streets were deserted, except for a familiar yellow dog followed by the hunchbacked beggar. Ripping the curtain a little more, Arnie made the tear larger so he could watch the beggar and his dog. He almost fell off of the bench when the beggar began to disappear from view.

"So what are you waiting for?" shouted the rabbi.

Arnie looked up. Willie had stopped chanting and it was his turn. "I—I lost my book," he said.

"Lost your book!" coughed the rabbi, opening the bottle of medicine again. He coughed so violently that he upset the glass of tea, spilling some onto himself.

Willie began to laugh.

"Troublemaker!" the rabbi shouted at Arnie. Arnie laughed nervously, and the rabbi smacked him on the head.

"I—I hate you!" shouted Arnie, as he ran to the door.

"Come back here, you troublemaker! Come back here! Do you hear me, Schiffman?"

"Safe," Arnie whispered to himself when he reached the hallway of his building. He went up the steps two at a time and pretended to be a blind man when he opened the door to the apartment—everything smelled like fried veal cutlets.

"Your magic wonder dog made on the floor again!" his mother shouted from the kitchen, above Houdini's barking. Arnie went directly to his room and stretched himself across the bed. Houdini pounced on top of him and nuzzled him, expecting a good wrestle. Instead, Arnie just held him close and stroked him. "You don't know what happened to me today," he said.

"Wait until your father hears about what your dog's been up to!" his mother shouted.

Arnie listened to the kitchen sounds and tried to imagine what his mother was doing. He heard the silverware clinking against the dishes. He knew she had put his father's setting down first at the head of the table. Arnie got an uneasy feeling about his father and he held Houdini close and kissed him. He pretended he told his father about how the rabbi had hit him and hurt him really bad, and how his father would say, "Okay, no more rabbi, no more bar mitzvah." Arnie began to think about different religions and what it would be like to worship Buddha. Images of friendly, big-bellied Buddhas came to Arnie. His imaginings were interrupted by the ringing of the doorbell.

"See who it is!" called his mother.

It was Gloria. "Hello, Arnold," she said, clutching a tin of bread crumbs.

"Who is it?" asked his mother.

"It's only Gloria," said Arnie.

"I'm returning the bread crumbs," Gloria explained.

Arnie went back into his room and closed the door.

"Arnold, I'm having a Halloween party Saturday and I'd like you to come," Gloria called through the door.

"I'm busy," shouted Arnie.

"I even invited Elliot Gold!" she shouted back.

Arnie went to the closet and reached under a big blanket for the box marked "trading cards." He closed his eyes and got a bouncy feeling in his heart hoping the box was there, undiscovered, exactly as he had left it. It was. Houdini sniffed the bird's nest, and Arnie picked up the clay rabbi doll. He heard footsteps at the bedroom door and quickly pushed everything under his bed. Houdini crawled under the bed too.

"Knock, knock! Anyone at home?" asked his mother, walking into the room with Gloria. "Arnie dear, it isn't polite to leave company, especially when they've just invited you to a party." She winked at Gloria, who giggled.

Arnie sat frozen, watching Houdini's tail

sticking out from under the bed, hoping he wouldn't back out with something in his mouth.

"Oh, what's that?" cried Gloria, rushing over to the half-completed production box.

"That's Arnie's magic cabinet," said Mrs. Schiffman. She spoke about his magic in a phony sweet voice. Arnie knew his mother hated his magic, and his building of the cabinet. She always complained about there being no room for his stuff. When he started work on the cabinet she nagged about the pieces of wood she found all over, and how the smell of the glue gave her a week-long headache. In front of other people she pretended to love the magic, but Arnie couldn't understand why she had to pretend in front of this creepy girl.

Gloria touched the cabinet. "Oh, it's all so mysterious!" she squealed.

"If she'd only take her fat fingers off of it," thought Arnie. He hated to have anyone but himself touch his magic equipment.

"How is it going to work?" asked Gloria, trying to pick it up.

"Be careful!" shouted Arnie. "It's not finished yet!"

Gloria put it down clumsily, and a section

fell off. "Oh, I'm sorry," she said. "I really am." Arnie could see that she really was sorry but he wanted to say something to really make her feel bad.

"That's all right, dear," said Mrs. Schiffman, seating herself on the bed. "Arnie doesn't mind."

Arnie does mind, Arnie does mind, Arnie does mind, he thought clenching his fists. "Oh, it's good to sit," said Mrs. Schiffman. "I don't know what's come over me lately, but I get so tired."

Arnie wished they'd both get out of his room. Most of the time, Arnie felt that it wasn't his room, because his mother always came in and told him what to do.

"I have a good idea," said Gloria. "You can come to my Halloween party dressed as a magician."

"No, thanks. Saturday I'm going someplace with my father."

"Sometimes, Arnie, I just think you're not normal," said his mother. "Maybe we should take you to a doctor."

Whenever she wanted to have her way, she pulled that line about his not being normal, and how a visit to the doctor might be necessary. Arnie hated doctors.

"I know your father would like you to go to a party with other children, rather than tagging along with him."

Arnie never thought of going with his father as tagging along. He was more like a good friend when they went someplace. His mother didn't understand anything!

"Gloria, of course Arnie will go to your party," said Mrs. Schiffman.

Arnie said nothing. When they left, Houdini came out from under the bed with a clay doll in his mouth. "Did you hear that? I have to go to that dumb jerk's crummy party."

Arnie took the voodoo doll from Houdini. He looked at it and wondered if he should make more of them, like for the tough kids, and Gloria—and maybe even his mother.

Arnie stuck another pin in the rabbi doll.

10. The Case of the Disappearing Rabbi

"It's either going to be *I Remember Mama,* or Dickens' *Christmas Carol.* I haven't reached a decision yet."

Miss Noonan began to talk about the Christmas play and how she expected everyone to be a part of it. About the only time Arnie didn't mind listening to Miss Noonan was when she talked about putting on plays.

"It's just for sissies," whispered Robert Berry, loud enough for some of the kids to hear. The boys laughed and Arnie laughed too. He really wanted to try out for a part, but the whispered remark suddenly made him feel uncertain.

Miss Noonan began to write history questions on the board. She interrupted herself to remind everyone that report cards weren't too far away. Arnie hated report cards as much as he hated all the tests that led up to them. There were always the explanations and promises of "I'll do better next time," when his father signed it.

Arnie watched two sparrows outside on the window ledge, and from the color of the sky behind them he knew it would soon be time to face the rabbi.

In the three o'clock schoolyard rush, Gloria ran alongside Arnie. "What are you going to wear to my party?" she asked.

"I thought I'd borrow your clothes and come as a clown." He ran ahead leaving Gloria behind in the crush. Walking to the rabbi's, he almost expected an ambush from the toughs. He knew he couldn't beat them all up, but he imagined how he would knock each one out at a time, and they'd never bother him again. As he neared the rabbi's he wondered if he should apologize to him, or not say anything about what had happened the other day.

When Arnie reached the rabbi's door he was surprised to find a note tacked to it which said "Lessons canceled." He felt like jumping up and shouting. As he walked away his happy feeling faded. Had something happened to the rabbi? The more Arnie thought about it, the more it bothered him. He wondered if the voodoo doll really had worked. Oh, probably the rabbi had to go to a wedding, or a funeral, or something.

To get his mind off the rabbi, he stopped and looked at a model railroad in the hobby shop window. But then he found himself looking at his own reflection. I wonder, he mused. I wonder.

Arnie wanted to go home and work on his production cabinet, but he didn't want to explain about not being at Hebrew school. He decided to walk around Freemont Avenue and look in the store windows.

Naked dress dummies looked out from the windows of Fyfe Bros. department store while they were being trimmed. Two girls ran past giggling. "Dopey girls," Arnie said to himself. "They're just models, and anyway, they don't even show anything."

Going inside the store, Arnie found it crowded with women shoppers. He wove his way through the ladies and counters and rode the escalator up to the second floor. Big red-white-and-blue signs announced the American Colonial Collection of furniture. He followed the signs and arrows to the room settings. A banner held by two wooden eagles was suspended above the exhibition entrance. Written on the banner in a fancy scroll was

"The American Dream House." Arnie walked under the banner and suddenly felt as if he was visiting people he didn't know. The cozy maple furniture with the plaid coverings seemed to belong to a family in which the father's name was Bill and the mother's Mary Ann. The two blond sons, Bill, Jr., and Jim, probably called their father "sir," and their mother called them "dears."

A large fireplace with fake logs burning in it caught Arnie's attention. He remained looking at it for a long time and thought it was almost as terrific as a good magic trick. A thin-mustached salesman in a bad-fitting suit walked by several times and looked at him suspiciously. Arnie got the idea that the salesman thought he was up to no good, so he left the fireplace and the room settings. He wondered why it always seemed that grown-ups think kids are going to get into trouble when they're not doing what grown-ups think they should be doing. Arnie made a face behind the salesman's back. And he wanted to tell him that his suit was crummy and that he had dandruff.

In another section of the same floor a

demonstration typewriter was attached to a desk, with a card reading "Just Try It." It didn't say anything about grown-ups or kids, so Arnie ripped a sheet of paper from his lesson book and sat down at the typewriter, and began to type. IIIII IIIIIIIIIIIIIIIIIIIII I I I you you you me mem em me crap crap crap carp crapppp rabbi rabbi rabbbi. After a whole page of just typing words, Arnie decided to write a story. He put a clean piece of paper in the typewriter and began.

The case of the dissapearing rabbi

All the boys realy new Rabbi Fyfe realy hated them. but it did'nt matter becuase thier mothers and fathers made themgo any way. He would blow his knose and wipe it on his sleeve and hisbreath smelled like Onyns and when he got mad whitch happened a lot he siad dirty things but that did'nt matter because theboys still had to go to him. He realy made kids wissh they were'nt jewish espesially Alan who he hated extraspesial . . . ! * " @ one day when Alan got toooo hebrew school he found a strang note onthe door. ₜhe rabbi never left a note befor

Arnie felt someone watching him, stopped

typing, and looked up. It was the thin-mustached salesman. Arnie quickly typed "to be
continued" on his paper, pulled it from the
typewriter, and left the store.

On the way home he tried to push thoughts
of the rabbi out of his head by wondering
what he should wear to Gloria's party.

11. Gloria's Party

He wrapped a bath towel around his head turban-style, and taped a black paper beard to his chin. Houdini looked at him strangely. "It's only me," laughed Arnie. "Do I really look like an Oriental magician?" Houdini jumped up on the bed barking.

Arnie didn't feel too bad about going to Gloria's party now, because he found out he wouldn't have been able to go with his father that day anyway. His father had to take his mother to the doctor.

He wasn't too sure he wanted to go to the party dressed as a magician. He thought about leaving the beard on and going as a rabbi, but he quickly got rid of that idea. "Rabbi Bliesch, where *are* you?" he shouted, pulling the beard from his chin.

Arnie searched the closets for a different costume. Houdini joined in, discovering that Arnie's mother's shoes were fun to chew. "Do you want to go to the party with me?" asked

Arnie, taking a shoe from Houdini. The dog looked at Arnie and cocked his head. "It's just at dopey Gloria's." Arnie sat cross-legged on the floor and put his arm around Houdini. "Hey, boy, what am I going to go as? I really want to fool 'em."

In the big cedar closet in his parents' room Arnie found a bundle of old clothing, some belonging to his father, some to his mother, and some to himself. While going through the old clothes, Arnie got his costume idea. He dressed in his father's old jacket and pants, and then tore a dress into strips and tied pieces of it around his legs. He put on an old pair of his father's shoes and pulled a hat down over his face, which he dirtied with some pastels. Arnie made a small bundle from his old clothing and stuffed it under his jacket like a hump.

Standing in front of the mirror he laughed and made crazy faces. "Just a dime for a poor old beggar," he said to Houdini in a cracked voice. Houdini put his tail between his legs and ran under a chair. Arnie laughed louder, pleased with his disguise. He twisted his face into a sinister expression and pointed to himself. "Rabbi killer!" he hissed. Arnie turned quickly from the mirror, having frightened himself.

Outside, children in costumes roamed the streets, trick or treating. Arnie, pretending to be the hunchbacked beggar, walked slowly with Houdini at his side. While Houdini sniffed around, he stood with his arm outstretched and his hand cupped as he'd seen the beggar do when asking for money. He could barely see past the brim of his hat.

Then he heard shouts of "It's the hunchback! It's the hunchback! Let's get 'im!" He pushed the hat brim back. It was the tough kids running toward him, twirling stockings filled with flour over their heads. Arnie grabbed Houdini and ran into Gold's grocery store.

"I'm sorry—not today," said Mr. Gold, coming from behind the counter.

"It's me, Mr. Gold!" said Arnie.

"Well, I'll be—" said Mr. Gold, rubbing his head. "How do you like that, Sylvie? It's Arnie Schiffman."

Mrs. Gold looked at Arnie closely. "You could have fooled me," she said, laughing.

Arnie waited until the coast was clear, and

then ran home—to Gloria's party. Going upstairs with Houdini, Arnie could hear Gloria
banging away at the piano. He was the last
to arrive at the party, and when he did everyone screamed, "It's the hunchback!" Some
girls locked themselves in the bathroom.

"You almost had me fooled, Arnold Schiffman," said Gloria. She was dressed as a gypsy,
and so were four other girls. Arnie thought
she looked older and almost pretty with her
mother's lipstick and eye makeup on.

"Where's Elliot?" he asked.

"Here I am," said Elliot, who was also
dressed as a gypsy. He wore a kerchief over
his head and he had on one of his mother's
old printed robes.

"You sure look sweet," said Arnie, laughing.

"Do you want your palm read?" asked
Elliot, and he grabbed Arnie's hand and
painted a red spot on it. "There! It's red."
Arnie wiped the spot off on Elliot's face.

"Cut it out!" said Gloria, "No rough-hous-
ing at my party." When she went back to the
piano, Arnie and Elliot squirted soda pop on
one of the girls. She ran crying into the bathroom.

"Arnie, keep it up, and I'm going to ask you to leave my party," said Gloria.

"Oh, she's just a poor sport," said Arnie.

"Hey, Arnie, why don't you do some magic tricks?" asked Elliot.

Arnie would have liked to entertain, but he thought it would be like showing off. "Nah, some other time," he said.

Gloria walked out of the kitchen with a bottle in her hand. "Time for you know what!" she said, giggling. "And the rules are, we have to go into the bedroom to kiss."

Charlie Levin, who was dressed as a pirate, was the first to spin, and he had to kiss Gloria's friend Debbie. They were in the room a long time and all the kids began to holler and Gloria banged on the door.

"Come on up for air," she shouted.

Charlie walked out of the room pretending to be exhausted. Everyone laughed. Debbie punched him on the arm, her face turned red and she said, "Nothing happened!"

Gloria spun the bottle and she had to kiss Arnie. Arnie made a face.

"Good luck!" shouted Elliot.

"Well, here goes nothing," said Arnie, going into the bedroom to kiss Gloria.

She moved away, saying "Ugh! Who wants to be kissed by a smelly old beggar!" And she ran out of the room.

Arnie felt disappointed, even if it was only Gloria.

"Boy! That was fast," said Elliot.

While the game continued, Arnie broke a balloon, and then Charlie broke one, and then all the kids were breaking balloons.

"Stop it!" cried Gloria, "Come on now, stop it!"

No one listened, and pretty soon all the decorations were down.

"It's all your fault, Arnold Schiffman!" Gloria screamed.

Arnie ran down to his apartment laughing. "That'll teach her," he said, rolling on the floor with Houdini.

12.   The Operation

Arnie's mother and father returned from the doctor's looking pale and red-eyed. They seemed different to him. They both moved slowly and almost ignored him. And when his mother did ask about the party, it was as if she was remembering something from long ago.

Houdini barked, and Arnie's mother put her hand over her face. Through muffled sobs she said, "That dog makes me so nervous!"

His father told him to take Houdini for a walk and gave him money for his dinner. "Have something in the delicatessen," he said, "Mother's not up to cooking tonight."

Arnie liked to eat in the delicatessen, it meant hot dogs with plenty of mustard and sauerkraut, and a cream soda. But the way things were, he didn't feel like eating. He went out anyway. And he knew something was really wrong when his mother didn't call out after him. "Go easy on the mustard and sauerkraut and drink your soda slowly," she would always say.

It was getting dark and a few jack-o'-lanterns glowed from windows. Arnie walked past the delicatessen, not even thinking about eating. He thought about his mother, and the rabbi, and how it was going to be when he was a great magician. "Things are going to work out," he said to Houdini. "Don't you think so?"

Sunday morning, whispered conversations took place between his mother and father. On most Sunday mornings, Arnie and his father would read Bible stories to each other from a large illustrated edition of the Old Testament, or play the farm game.

The farm game began when Arnie's father got to the real estate section of the newspaper. Then he and Arnie would read aloud the farms and acreage for sale, and when they came to one they liked they'd shout, "I'll buy that!" Arnie liked to read about all the stables, and horses, and lakes for sale. His father would often say, "Someday we'll really buy a farm and live the good life."

That Sunday, the Bible remained untouched and no one went to buy the newspapers. Even breakfast was different. The Sunday cup of coffee Arnie was allowed was never brewed. When he asked, "What's wrong?" his father answered, "Mother's not feeling well."

The Sunday afternoon stillness that invaded the apartment was broken only by the ticking of the clock and the sobbing of his mother. He remained in his room. Unable to do his homework, he sat idly twisting the rubber chicken until it tore. His father came in and suggested that Arnie might enjoy going to the movies. Most of the time he liked going to the movies, but now this, too, was something he didn't feel like doing. His father insisted, so he went.

The usherette made Arnie sit all the way over on the side in the children's section of the theater, even though there were just a few grown-ups in the adult section. It was warm and stuffy inside the theater and the girl sitting next to him smelled of stale milk. Besides, he was really mad at the candy counter lady who sold him chocolate covered nuts when he asked for chocolate covered raisins, and when he tried to return them because he said he hated nuts, she said, "We don't exchange, and anyway that's what you asked for." Arnie made a trail of candy down the aisle when he went back to his seat.

He hardly paid attention to the main feature which seemed pretty dopey to him. It was all about a man and woman who had bad timing. Like she got to the airport just when his plane was leaving, and he got to the train station just as her train was pulling out, and then at the end they got together by accident in the same taxi.

During the intermission Arnie put the empty candy box in the toilet bowl with lots of paper, hoping to stuff it up. The second feature was all about a Chinese detective who gets on a freighter with spies, ancient treasure, and secret scrolls. Arnie liked the action parts, which always happened in lots of fog.

When Arnie left the movie his head ached, and as he got nearer to home he began to think about his mother and he felt a little sick. He almost wished, now, that the movie wasn't over, so he wouldn't have to go home.

Houdini greeted Arnie at the door by jumping up on him as usual. The apartment was dark except for a small lamp in his parents' bedroom. His mother was asleep, and his father was sitting quietly in the darkened living room. Arnie noticed a suitcase at the foot of his mother's bed.

In the morning, when Arnie was leaving for school, his mother did something she had never done before. She held him and kissed him, and with a forced smile she said, "Be a good boy." She gave him money for school lunch, which was also something she had never done before.

It was hard for Arnie to pay attention in class. Miss Noonan scolded him for not doing his homework, when he couldn't answer a question. She told the class that the play she had decided upon was *I Remember Mama*. She gave out copies of the play to several kids in the class. "Don't jump to any conclusions," she said. "I just want some of you to familiarize yourselves with the play—this isn't for casting." Arnie wanted a copy real bad, but he didn't get one.

At lunchtime Arnie sat in the empty schoolyard instead of eating. The afternoon sun made strong shadows in the schoolyard, and the one made by the flagpole seemed miles long. He thought about the man and the lady in the movie who kept missing each other because of bad timing, and how some people always seemed to catch the right train. He thought of Gordon Rosewell, one of the boys in his class who got a copy of the play. He'd never miss a train, thought Arnie, who envied and disliked him. Gordon's honey-colored hair was always in place, and even when they played tag and it got mussed up it still looked right. He thought of Gordon's mother, who was young and had pretty blue eyes and often baked cookies for the whole class. And whom Miss Noonan called by her first name.

A cloud moved in front of the sun and all the shadows disappeared, making the schoolyard appear even more deserted. Arnie found himself wishing that the rabbi would be there that afternoon, and that when he got home the apartment would smell of cooking. He suddenly got hungry for chocolate pudding, and remembered the time he was sick and home from school, and his mother let him lick the pot clean after she made the pudding.

Arnie tried not to cry. "Mama, I'll be good," he whispered.

The dreary afternoon class routine was broken by an outburst of crying when Beatrice Schildkraut discovered ink spots on her new blouse. Arnie was happy about the disruption, but he felt sorry for Beatrice. She was an okay girl, and he felt bad that the whole class saw her cry.

Miss Noonan went into a long thing about how to remove ink from different fabrics. Arnie thought how great it would be if she could just give up teaching and open a cleaning store. Beatrice's blouse occupied his thoughts for a while—he wondered how the entire blouse would look with ink spots, or if the whole thing should be ink color. At the three o'clock bell, thoughts of Beatrice's blouse shattered, and a terrible, familiar feeling returned to Arnie.

As he approached the rabbi's he could see the piece of paper still tacked to the front door. He went up to read it once again, but the message remained unchanged: "Lessons canceled." Arnie sat down on a step, in hopes that the door would open and the rabbi would stick his head out and say, "Okay, you can come in now!" But the door remained closed. He looked in above the curtained part of the window. It was dark inside. He began to wonder if there really were people with special magic powers that made voodoo dolls work, and was he one of them? "But God wouldn't let anything happen to a rabbi," he told himself.

Walking aimlessly, Arnie found himself standing in front of Fyfe Bros. department store. The window dummies were now dressed in warm winter clothes, and white powder looking like snow was sprinkled around their feet. The snow reminded Arnie of the times he went sleigh-riding in his old neighborhood and the fun he'd had. It suddenly made Arnie wonder what happened to his sled—he hadn't seen it since the move. He wanted to run home and ask where it was.

Instead, he walked into the store and rode the escalator up to the second floor and went directly to the typewriter. This time he avoided the furniture display and the chance of seeing the same salesman again. He sat down at the typewriter and began again:

> even thouh all thekids at hebrew school hated the rabbi they began to wonder waht happened to him. Someone siad something terible happened because he did'nt believe in God and God new he was a foney. God knows when some one is truthful or not espesially when someone is working forhim like the rabbi.

He stopped typing and thought about his story. He looked around and there, wearing the same rotten-fitting suit, was the salesman. Arnie got his belongings together and went home.

Opening the front door, Arnie got an awful feeling. The apartment was quiet and Houdini wasn't there to greet him. He saw his father at the end of the long hallway and he knew something was wrong. His father was never home that early.

"Where's Houdini?" he cried.

His father looked tired and worried. "Come here, Arnie—we have to talk," he said softly. Arnie knew that every time his father said, "We have to talk," something was wrong or something awful would happen.

"I don't want to talk," shouted Arnie, frightened and trembling. "Where's Houdini?"

"Arnie, Mother's in the hospital. She's very sick—please try to understand."

"Where's Houdini?" he asked again.

"I had to give him away." His father sighed deeply.

"You can't give him away! He's mine and I want him!" Arnie broke into tears, and through heavy sobs he continued shouting, "I want him, I want him!"

"You'll be going to stay with Aunt Fran and Uncle Henry for a while. And things will have to be different when Mother comes home."

"I don't care! I don't care! I want Houdini back!"

"I gave him to a man at work who has a big backyard, and he'll be happy, and—"

"I want him back!" cried Arnie, his face wet and his eyes burning.

"Sometimes we have to do things we don't want to do."

Arnie didn't listen. He ran into his bedroom and buried his face in the pillow. The next morning, before Arnie left, he tore the bird's nest apart and threw it in the garbage.

13. *The Terrible Visit*

Sniffling and red-eyed, Arnie sat next to Aunt Fran on the bus. She tried to comfort him by saying that his cousin Susan had planned some fun things for them to do. She also said that she was sure he'd get another dog as soon as his mother was better.

"But I don't want another dog," he sobbed. "I just want Houdini back."

Aunt Fran gave him her handkerchief, and he made it so wet that he was ashamed to give it back to her. They got off the bus, and the cold evening pinched at his face, making it hurt. He put his hands to his cheeks.

"We'll be there soon," said Aunt Fran, walking close to Arnie. As they neared the house, Susan and Amy waved to them from a window. The house looked friendly, with the lighted windows and his cousins waving. When they went inside Susan and Amy greeted Arnie with hugs and kisses.

"I'm sorry, Arn," Susan whispered into his ear.

"Me too," said Amy. Arnie tried to be brave in front of his cousins. He didn't want them to see him cry, but he cried anyway. Arnie's grandmother came into the room clasping her hands, and shaking her head back and forth as Arnie had seen the old people do in the synagogue.

"Oh God, be good to my child," she said, looking up at the ceiling. She hugged Arnie so tightly that her glasses fell to the floor. "You'll have to pray hard for your mother, Arnie!" she cried.

"I gotta go to the bathroom, Bubba," he said, holding back a new set of tears. He locked himself in, and stayed there for a long time.

"Arn, are you all right?" called Susan, knocking on the bathroom door.

Arnie looked at the flamingos on the shower curtains and then at the glass shelf with all the bubble-bath powders. He took a deep breath. The room smelled sweet, too sweet. It made Arnie dizzy. He got the feeling that the whole thing had happened once before. Susan's voice seemed far away, and when he half closed his eyes everything looked blurry, like a too-wet watercolor painting.

"My father's home," Susan called. "Time for supper!"

Arnie opened the bathroom door.

"Feel a little better?" she asked.

Arnie shook his head yes, but he was just pretending.

"What a good surprise!" said Uncle Henry, messing up Arnie's hair.

"We have your favorite," said Aunt Fran. "Roast chicken and cranberry sauce."

"And I made the dessert," said Susan.

"I made it too!" said Amy.

He hardly touched his food, and even the dessert of raspberry Jell-o with whipped cream remained untouched.

After the table was cleared everyone sat in the living room. Aunt Fran told Arnie how all arrangements had been made with the school, and his father would contact Miss Noonan and phone in the homework assignments.

"And I can help you," said Susan, always trying to make Arnie feel extra good. She also asked Arnie if he wanted to play Monopoly or use her typewriter. Arnie shook his head no. "I know!" she said. "How would you like to listen to my new record album?" and before Arnie had a chance to answer she went to get it.

While the record played, Arnie could hear pieces of conversation between Aunt Fran, Uncle Henry, and his grandmother. He kept hearing the words—operation, malignant, benign—over and over again.

A room downstairs at Bubba's had been prepared for him. Before going to sleep that night his grandmother said, "You'll pray hard for your mother, and with God's help she'll be all right." While his grandmother snored in the next room, Arnie lay awake thinking. He wondered if terrible things were happening because God was punishing him for not listening to his mother, and taking home the bird's nest from the cemetery. And for making voodoo dolls, and for telling the rabbi he hated him. But he hit me, thought Arnie.

He finally fell asleep as the sky began to grow light, and he dreamed about Houdini.

"The operation was successful and everything is going to be all right," said Aunt Fran, handing the phone to Arnie. He listened as his father told him that his mother was all right, that he should be a good boy, and that he would see him soon with a surprise. Arnie asked what the surprise was, but his father only said, "It'll be a good one. I'll see to that."

"My father said he has a surprise for me," said Arnie.

"Maybe you'll get Houdini back," said Amy. Susan kicked Amy's shoe.

During the week, when Aunt Fran and Uncle Henry visited the hospital, they took with them get-well cards which Arnie had made for his mother. They also brought back messages from his mother.

"Your mother's worried about you," said Aunt Fran. "But your Uncle Henry told her that you're a big boy. He reminded her that you're on your way to bar mitzvah." Arnie felt his ears get warm like the times when he was caught in a lie. He tried not to look at Aunt Fran.

"I can't wait until your bar mitzvah," said Amy. "I'm going to wear the prettiest dress in the whole world."

During the day, when Susan and Amy were

away at school, Arnie watched his grandmother do the cooking. "You can be my official
taster," she said, always giving him samples
from the many pots on top of the stove. While
she cooked she told stories about the old country, and people she had known who were now
gone. "They should only rest well," she would
say. She told him about the hardships and the
struggle to get to America, and what a miracle
it was to have heat and hot water and a stove
to cook with.

Arnie watched his grandmother, thin and
bent, stirring a pot with a large wooden spoon.
She had become someone he didn't know, as
she told her stories from another time. "How
about another taste?" she'd say, holding out the
wooden spoon to him. Everything Bubba
cooked was always delicious. Arnie knew it
was her special touch, not just the ingredients,
that made things good.

One night Arnie asked Susan if she would
let him use her typewriter. "Dopey, you know
you can use it anytime," she said giving it to
Arnie. Arnie sat at his Uncle Henry's desk and
began to type.

dear Houdini

 i sure misss you. i hope you are havnig
fun in your new back yard. do you miss
me ? ? ? ? ?

"What are you typing?" asked Amy, resting
her elbows on the desk.

"A letter," said Arnie.

"To who?" she asked.

"To a good friend," said Arnie.

"Are you doing your homework?" asked
Aunt Fran.

"No," said Arnie.

"You'd better," warned Aunt Fran, "or
you'll fall behind your class."

Arnie stopped typing and pretended to
study his schoolwork, but his mind was on
other things. He thought about Houdini, and
about why his father hadn't said anything
about Hebrew lessons and the rabbi. He also
thought about the class play. And he wondered if operations hurt an awful lot.

14. Grand Jeté

Arnie watched the snow fall on the capitol building and when it settled he shook the paperweight again. As he waited for Susan and Amy to get ready, he tried to cough loud and long enough for Aunt Fran to think he was sick and tell him that he didn't have to go to dance class with Susan and Amy. Arnie who was usually great at faking coughs was having trouble getting a good one started.

It was Aunt Fran's idea about Arnie's seeing the ballet class, and Susan and Amy thought it was a good one. "I'm sure you'll find it very interesting," they said. He didn't want to hurt anyone's feelings, so he didn't say anything about not wanting to go.

Aunt Fran gave Susan money to hold for lunch in a restaurant afterward. On the bus, Susan and Amy argued as to who would sit next to Arnie. Susan gave in to Amy, saying, "Well, sometimes little children must have their way." And she made Amy hold the dance bag.

"Wait until you meet Mr. Petrokoff," said Susan.

"Who's Mr. Petrokoff?" asked Arnie.

"Oh, he's our dance teacher," said Amy.

"And one of the greatest in the world," said Susan.

"Susan's got a crush on him," said Amy.

"Oh, shut up, stupid, I do not!" said Susan, turning and looking out the window. Amy stuck her tongue out at Susan. Girls can sure be dopey, Arnie thought to himself.

On the street, Susan and Amy quarreled as to who should carry the dance bag. At one point they just dropped it and walked away. Arnie said he'd carry it, but he really didn't mean it. Amy ran back and picked it up. "Wait until I tell Mother!" she threatened.

They walked to the dancing school with Arnie in the middle. A stray dog ran past, and he got an awful feeling. He bit the inside of his cheek hoping to prevent the tears, but it didn't help. Susan and Amy noticed but they didn't say anything—they just looked at each other.

"Here we are," said Susan, stopping in front of a shoe store.

"It looks like a shoe store to me," said Arnie.

"No, upstairs, silly," said Amy pointing.

He looked up. Above the store were large windows painted with leaping silhouettes of dancers. "Why don't I wait down here?" he asked, feeling funny about going up to the dance school.

"Arnie, come on," said Susan. "No one is going to bite you."

The dance studio was a large mirrored room with a piano and some chairs lined up in front of the windows. "Just take a seat," said Susan, going off with Amy to change clothes. Some girls and a boy were doing exercises at a bar. A pink-faced man with a long scarf sat at the piano reading a newspaper. Arnie squirmed uncomfortably on the metal folding chair, and it made creaking noises. A blond curly-headed man wearing black tights entered the room. Arnie wanted to laugh, but he held it back. The man nodded to everyone and Arnie was surprised that he nodded to him too. He smiled back nervously.

After the blond man spoke to the man at the piano he walked over to Arnie. "And what have we here—a new student?" he asked, extending his hand toward Arnie.

"No, I'm going to be a magician," said Arnie. The man smiled, showing lots of white, white teeth. Arnie smiled back with his mouth shut, because he remembered he had forgotten to brush his teeth that morning. "I'm just here because of Susan and Amy," he said, keeping his lips stiff when he spoke. "They're my cousins."

Susan and Amy returned dressed in black leotards. Arnie thought Susan looked extra special in her dance outfit.

"Mr. Petrokoff, this is our cousin Arnold," said Susan. She spoke more grown-up and Arnie knew she was trying to put on a show for Mr. Petrokoff.

"There's a family resemblance," said Mr. Petrokoff. "He has the same color eyes as you."

Arnie became aware of his eyes, and he tried hard to keep from blinking. He also continued to keep his lips stiff to prevent his unbrushed teeth from showing.

"Don't you feel good?" whispered Amy.

Arnie shook his head no, and began to blink. The room filled up with more kids in leotards, and Arnie was surprised to see some more boys among them.

Mr. Petrokoff clapped his hands, and the pink-faced man at the piano folded his newspaper, sat on it, and began to play. The kids lined up at the bar and Mr. Petrokoff shouted instructions. "Stretch, stretch, stretch!" The class stretched up and down.

Arnie wanted to laugh, but he knew if he did it would just mean trouble, so he began to think about sad things, and a real sadness came over him.

"Center work!" said Mr. Petrokoff. With those instructions the entire class lined up in formations in the middle of the room. Amy smiled, and Susan winked at Arnie. He smiled back and his sadness began to leave him as he watched the class work.

"Okay, class, cross floor!" shouted Mr. Petrokoff. "Grand jeté!" One by one the class leaped across the room.

Arnie sat on the edge of his chair, almost eager to join in. The man at the piano played harder, and Arnie noticed that his glasses were resting on the tip of his nose.

"Grand jeté!" said Mr. Petrokoff, leaping across the room several times. "Arms like this! Legs like this!" Arnie had never seen anyone do that before and it seemed like the closest thing to flying.

After the lesson was over everyone left the room to change. Arnie stood in front of the mirror. "Grand jeté!" he said, and began leaping across the room.

"Very good," said Mr. Petrokoff, who had returned to the room.

Arnie stopped, and felt his face grow warm until it reached the tips of his ears, which almost burned.

"Are you sure you want to be a magician?"

After they left the class, Amy asked, "What were you and Mr. Petrokoff talking about?"

"Oh, nothing," said Arnie.

"Arnie, you're lying," said Amy.

"Okay, we spoke about how great you dance."

"Oh, phooey!" said Amy. Susan laughed.

As they walked along the shop-lined street, Susan and Amy kept stopping to look in windows. Arnie decided that the next time they stopped he would play a trick on them. When they passed a toy shop Susan and Amy rushed to the window and began to whisper to each other, ignoring Arnie. He walked on ahead and pretended to look in the window of a clothing store. Then he hid behind a mirrored column at the entranceway. He chuckled to himself, making believe his reflection was a friend who was in on the plot.

After a while, Arnie's stomach growled. "Time to eat," he said, leaving his hiding post. When he looked down the street the girls weren't anywhere in sight. Arnie got scared and raced up and down the street looking for them. Then he walked up and down, wondering what had happened to them and what he should do. And just as he thought about going back to the dance school he heard his name being called. Susan and Amy were coming out of the toy shop carrying a package. He ran to them.

"Arnie, we hope you didn't think we were pulling a rotten stunt when we disappeared into the toy shop," said Susan.

"But we had to, because we wanted to get you something," said Amy.

"It means going without lunch," said Susan, "but we wanted you to have it."

They handed Arnie the package. His stomach grumbled as he opened it. He almost cried when he saw what was in the box. It was a white dog. Arnie held it up to his face and closed his eyes, and for a moment it almost seemed real. "Girls sure are dopey," he said, and thanked them.

"Did you wonder where we were?" asked Amy.

"Oh, I figured you were playing games and hiding from me," said Arnie, feeling foolish about his prank.

When they got home, Arnie's father was there. "Daddy! Daddy!" Arnie cried, running into his father's arms.

His father hugged him. "Mother's home," he said, "and I've come to take you back."

"I've got all your things packed," said Aunt Fran. "Here's a special banana cake," said Bubba, kissing Arnie and handing him a brown package.

Susan and Amy looked as if they were going to cry when they said good-bye. And Uncle Henry said that if he ever had a son he wished he'd be just like Arnie.

On the way home Arnie asked his father

about the surprise he had mentioned on the phone. "Oh, you'll find it at home," said his father, and then asked if he had done all of his homework. He also told Arnie that the day he had called the rabbi to tell him about his absence, the rabbi wasn't in. "I'll write him a note when you go back," he added. The image of the note tacked to the rabbi's door came to Arnie.

Arnie shuddered, and changed the subject. He asked if the man at work was taking good care of Houdini, and if he could see him soon.

"Sure!" said his father.

Arnie looked out of the bus window, but all he saw were the images inside of his head. Miss Noonan and Gordon Rosewell, the rabbi, Gloria, Elliot, his mother, and Mr. Petrokoff doing great leaps.

They stopped at a florist on the way home and Arnie bought his mother a rose.

For a moment before the door to the apartment was opened, Arnie crossed his fingers and closed his eyes. "Please let Houdini be here," he whispered. But the apartment was quiet, and Arnie sighed at the letdown.

He felt as if he was in a tiptoe-and-whisper

apartment, a place that belonged to other people. He walked into his parents' bedroom and found his mother sitting up in bed. She looked different—her hair was combed back in a way he had never seen before. He was afraid to touch her, as he gave her the rose. She smiled and took his hand and kissed him on the forehead. Then she rubbed her hands alongside Arnie's face.

"You need a haircut," she whispered.

15. Picture-Taking

The radiator hissed and the smell of fresh coffee filled the apartment. A white-gray light filtered through the steamy windows of Arnie's room. He got out of bed to feed the turtle on the windowsill—it was the surprise from his father.

"Sunday breakfast!" he said, dropping a lot of dried insects into the bowl. The turtle's head and legs disappeared. "I think I'll call you Houdini, Jr., with that kind of disappearing act," said Arnie. Oh, how he missed Houdini.

"Breakfast! Come and get it!" shouted his father.

His mother joined them at the table. She was wearing lipstick and her hair was combed as he remembered it. "You look better already," he said.

"I feel better," his mother laughed. "The hospital was no picnic."

"I'll help you with everything," said Arnie.

"My good-looking little boy is growing up," she said. "Before you know it it will be bar mitzvah time." The mouthful of scrambled eggs Arnie had just eaten seemed to be stuck in his throat. He started to cough. "It's my fault," said his mother. "We shouldn't talk while we eat—it's bad for digestion."

His mother went back to bed, and Arnie helped his father with the dishes.

"I wish my bar mitzvah was over with," said Arnie.

"Then what will you wish for?" asked his father.

Arnie shrugged, without answering. After the dishes were done, he sat thinking about Houdini.

"Do you want to buy some property?" Arnie's father asked.

In the afternoon Arnie decided to visit Elliot. Elliot's room was different—it was full of photographic equipment.

"Wow! What's all this stuff?" asked Arnie.

"I think I'm going to be a photographer," said Elliot.

Arnie looked at the fuzzy photographs tacked to the wall. "I took those myself," said Elliot proudly, "and I developed them too."

"Hey, that's great!" said Arnie, examining Elliot's camera.

"Why don't we go out and take some pictures now, and we can come back and develop them ourselves," said Elliot.

"Will you let me take some pictures?" asked Arnie.

"Sure," said Elliot. "You can take them all if you like."

They walked for blocks trying to decide what to take pictures of. "Why don't I take a picture of you?" said Arnie finally.

Elliot made a scary face. "I'm a ghost," he said.

Arnie snapped the picture. "Now let's take pictures of the haunted house."

"But it's just an old broken-down house," said Elliot.

"Yeh, but it could be fun. You aren't afraid, are you?"

"Are you kidding?" laughed Elliot.

They walked along the canals in back of the mills. Brown leaves from nearby trees were thick in the water, making it appear almost solid. "How would you like to go swimming in that?" asked Elliot.

"Not on your life!" said Arnie.

They knelt at the canal's edge, testing its temperature with their fingers. "Yikes, it's cold!" shouted Arnie, blowing on his fingers.

"You can say that again," said Elliot, putting his hands between his thighs and pressing his legs together.

"What are you doing, goosing yourself up?" laughed Arnie.

"I'll goose *you* up!" Elliot laughed, and began to chase Arnie. They ran along the canal until they were out of breath. "Let's sit a minute," said Elliot, breathing heavily. "It's hard to run in this dumb coat."

"I could run faster too, if I wasn't wearing a coat and a sweater," said Arnie. Arnie didn't know whether he should tell Elliot about the rabbi's disappearance. "Do you believe in voodoo dolls?" he began cautiously.

"You mean like when you want something bad to happen to someone and you make a doll that looks like him and stick pins in it?"

"Yeh, do you believe in it?"

"I don't know, I think you have to have some kind of special magic to do that," said Elliot.

"Well, what if someone did and—" Arnie cut himself short because he was afraid Elliot would think he was crazy. He aimed the camera at his feet and pressed the button.

"Hey! What are you doing?" yelled Elliot.

"I'm taking a picture of my feet," said Arnie.

"What are you, crazy? Don't waste the film —there'll be nothing left for the haunted house," said Elliot. "We'd better hurry before it gets too dark."

The house was big, with turrets and spires and little balconies. A crumbling porch was wrapped around the house, and in place of front steps there were wooden crates piled on top of each other.

"Do you know, it's really kind of beautiful," said Arnie.

"Now I know you're crazy," said Elliot. "They say some guy hanged himself in the attic."

"Come on, let's explore it," said Arnie.

"I thought you only wanted to take pictures of it," said Elliot.

"Boy, if you aren't chicken!" said Arnie.

"Baloney," said Elliot, trying to sound tough.

They climbed the crates onto the porch. The large front door had once been stained glass—now all that remained was twisted pieces of lead. The porch was carpeted with fragments of colored glass. "Knock, knock! Is anyone home?" called Elliot, putting his head through a large opening in the door. "Be-waaarrrrrre!" moaned Arnie, grabbing at Elliot's waist.

Elliot quickly pulled his head out of the door opening. "Hey, cut it out! You almost gave me a heart attack," he said.

They entered the house, Arnie going first.

"It's cold in here and it smells like pee," whispered Elliot.

"Maybe ghosts don't know how to use the toilet," said Arnie.

"You mean they just pee all over everything?" asked Elliot, holding his nose. "Ugh, that's awful!"

"Say, ghostie, didn't your mommy ever potty-train you?" Arnie shouted. They began to laugh.

Suddenly they heard a noise in the house.

Arnie felt his head tighten. They stood close to each other. A shadow crossed the room. As they ran out of the house Arnie turned around and saw the hunchbacked shape of the beggar. They jumped off of the porch, and a dog began to bark.

"That sounds like Houdini," said Arnie.

"Are you nuts? All dogs sound alike," said Elliot.

"We didn't take any pictures!" said Arnie.

"You and your smart ideas about haunted houses," said Elliot.

"Well, how was I supposed to know the beggar lived there? But it sure is funny how much his dog sounded like Houdini."

16. *Understudy*

Miss Noonan greeted Arnie like an old friend, and she told Arnie how sorry she was to hear of his mother's illness. Her sweetness made him feel uncomfortable, and he wondered why something bad had to happen before she acted nice.

"We begin rehearsals in the auditorium today," she said. "While you were away, Arnold, I decided that you would be the perfect curtain puller."

Arnie supposed that this was still Miss Noonan's way of being nice, but he really didn't want to be the curtain puller. He felt like telling her to pull the curtain herself.

"It's an important job," she said. "A cue too early or too late can ruin a whole scene." Arnie hated to be sold something he didn't care about, and Miss Noonan's pushing the curtain job made him really not want it.

In the auditorium Arnie sat backstage on a stool. He ran his finger along the red velvet curtain and thought about being a great magician with audiences cheering wildly.

"Close the curtain, Arnold Schiffman, that's a cue!" shouted Miss Noonan. Arnie pulled the curtain closed. "Now, you'll have to study your cue sheet, Arnold, and pay strict attention!" said Miss Noonan, losing a little of her fake sweetness and sounding more like her old self.

"I really don't think I'm a good curtain puller," said Arnie.

"Nonsense, you'll be fine," said Miss Noonan.

He was afraid that on the day of the performance he'd really mess everything up, and then Miss Noonan would hate him for sure.

As it neared three o'clock, Miss Noonan told him he could be the blackboard monitor. Some kids thought being blackboard monitor was a big deal, but Arnie just wanted to be left alone. Especially today, when he was in a hurry to get to Hebrew school.

When the boards were wet they looked black and shiny, and when they began to dry they looked like the same rotten old gray blackboards. Arnie thought they should be called grayboards. On the way out, Miss Noonan said to him, "Arnold, try to apply yourself."

He ran all the way to Hebrew school, and he wanted to laugh out loud with relief when he saw the note missing from the door. He rang the bell and waited nervously for the door to open. When it did he was surprised to see a nice-looking young man standing there.

"Hello. I'm Rabbi Marks," he said, extending his hand.

Arnie shook hands. "I'm Arnie Schiffman."

"Of course," smiled the rabbi.

Because he was recognized, Arnie was now certain that something had happened to Rabbi Bliesch. "Rabbi killer," he said to himself.

"Rabbi Bliesch wasn't feeling well, so he went to Miami for a while, and I'll be your rabbi until he returns."

Arnie sighed with relief. "Oh, great! Oh, really great!" he said.

Willie gave Arnie a big greeting. He told Arnie that the day he had run out, the rabbi had announced that the lessons would be canceled for a few days, because he had planned a trip to Miami.

The new rabbi was nice and he used words like please and thank you, and when the lessons were over he said, "See you tomorrow," and gave out sticks of chewing gum. It was good to know all rabbis weren't like Rabbi Bliesch.

Instead of going directly home Arnie stopped off at Fyfe Bros. department store and typed: CaSE cLOSED RABBI FUOND

Arnie learned his curtain cues, as well as everyone's part. Some nights, he locked himself in the bathroom and played all the parts in front of the mirror. One night he heard his father say, "We've got a Doctor Jekyll and Mr. Hyde in our bathroom."

His mother was her old self again, and she told Arnie he'd better get out of the bathroom and straighten his room up.

The day of the costume fittings Gordon Rosewell did not come to school. His mother had called and said he was sick. The news made Arnie happy, and Miss Noonan miserable. That day she complained about everything and she said the costumes were awful.

The girls who had worked on them were almost in tears.

The next day, when Mrs. Rosewell called again about Gordon's absence, Miss Noonan almost had a fit. During rehearsal she let Arnie fill in for Gordon and was surprised to find that he knew the part. Unhappily, she gave the role of Nils to Arnie, and Robert Berry took over the job of curtain puller.

Arnie rehearsed on stage in the costume now fitted to him. He really liked the part, and all the kids told him they thought he was great. He was really excited, and his mother and father promised to come see him in the play.

But then Gordon Rosewell returned to class, and Miss Noonan greeted him with a hug and a kiss. "The real Nils has returned," she said. "But, class, let us thank Arnold Schiffman for his fine cooperation." She had a way of saying Arnie's name that made him want to change it. But he was sure if he had changed his name to Peter Potter, she would make it come out sounding the same way. He went back to his old job of curtain puller.

At that moment Arnie hated Miss Noonan

and Gordon Rosewell more than he had ever hated any two people in his whole life. He considered making voodoo dolls again.

The night of the performance the auditorium was filled to the last row, but Arnie spotted his mother and father. When the lights dimmed he pulled the curtain open slowly as he had been told to do. He didn't miss one curtain cue, although he was tempted to.

After the play Arnie's mother and father told him what a good job he had done.

"I really made a good Nils," he told them.

"I'm sure you did," they said.

17. No Christmas Presents, Please!

A light snow fell, and Arnie walked to school carrying a Christmas present for Miss Noonan. It was a box of handkerchiefs his mother had neatly wrapped. It was the last day of school before the Christmas vacation, and for days the kids had been talking about the presents they were getting for Miss Noonan. Arnie hated the whole idea of it because it gave some kids a chance to really show off.

When his mother wrapped the handkerchiefs, she said, "It's not the gift that counts, it's the thought behind it." Arnie didn't think Miss Noonan deserved anything except a rotten apple.

"Hi, Arnie," said Gloria coming up behind him. "Whatcha got in the box?" Gloria knew very well what was in the box—she just wanted him to ask what was in hers. "I'll tell you what I have, if you tell me what you have."

"I've got compressed vomit in mine, and I don't care what you have in yours," he said.

"Grump! Where's your Christmas spirit?" she asked.

"There!" said Arnie, tossing the box into a garbage pail.

The class sang Christmas carols and Miss Noonan handed out candy canes to everyone. "Now it's our turn to give you something," said Rita Nadel, acting as class spokesman. Miss Noonan faked surprise as all the kids ran around her desk with their gifts. Arnie went to the bathroom. He was sorry he had thrown the gift away, but he was also sorry his mother had even bought one.

At the end of the day when it was time to leave Miss Noonan made a speech and warned them that when the Christmas vacation was over they would all have to work hard to prepare for graduation.

"And if you want to qualify for the rapid advance class in Junior High, you'd better work extra hard." Arnie caught Miss Noonan looking directly at him. He had always done well in school, but this year his grades had fallen.

Outside, the snow was falling and Arnie was happy. The beginning of things always seemed like the best part, and this was the beginning of Christmas vacation. It was also the Jewish holiday of Chanukah, and Hebrew school was to be closed also. Arnie blew at the snowflakes and his walk turned to a slide as he pretended to ice-skate through the snow.

When he reached home and had barely taken his coat off, Gloria stopped by for a visit. "I thought Arnie would like to go skating with me tomorrow," she said to his mother, loud enough for him to hear.

"I'm sure he would, dear," said his mother.

"I'm busy!" shouted Arnie.

Gloria walked into his room and showed him the box of handkerchiefs hidden among some magazines she was carrying. "You are?" she said. "That's too bad!" She waved the box of handkerchiefs. Arnie tried to grab the box from her, but she ran to the front door. "See you tomorrow!" she called.

"Hey, wait for me!" shouted Gloria. "It's slippery, and I can't walk!"

"Get off the path and walk in the snow, like I'm doing," said Arnie.

"No—I'll get all wet!" cried Gloria.

"This was your idea, not mine, Miss Blackmail," said Arnie, running ahead. "I'll meet you at the lake."

"Rat!" she yelled.

"If I'm a rat, then you're Queen Rat!" he shouted back.

Arnie liked the sound of the snow crunching beneath his feet as he ran through the park. When he got to the lake he quickly put on his extra socks, laced up his skates tightly, and ran onto the ice. The lake reminded him of a Christmas card. The trees had snow all over them, and everyone on the lake seemed to be having fun.

"Arnold Schiffman, help me!"

He laughed when he saw Gloria waddling onto the ice with her skates untied. "The least you could do is tie my skates!" she cried.

Arnie knelt and tied her skates. "You must be wearing a hundred pairs of socks, or else you've got the fattest ankles in the world," said Arnie, putting his hands into his pockets. "My fingers are frozen."

"Let's hold hands and skate together," said Gloria.

"S-W-E-L-L!" moaned Arnie.

She took his hand. "Don't go fast now," she warned. She skated like a wobbly sack and fell down, taking him with her. He heard someone laughing—it was Elliot with his camera.

"That's the first time I've seen a skating beanbag," he shouted. Leaving Gloria, Arnie skated over to him.

"Do you want to take pictures?" asked Elliot.

"Sure," said Arnie, who had had enough of skating with Gloria. He took off his skates, and he and Elliot started running.

"Come back here!" shouted Gloria, who kept falling down and was dripping wet. "Okay for you!"

"Good-bye, Gloria!" yelled Arnie.

"And good riddance," added Elliot.

They ran through the snow throwing snowballs at each other, and then rolled around in it until the tips of their noses burned.

"Let's go back to the haunted house," said Arnie.

"Haven't you had enough of that place?" asked Elliot.

"But we didn't take pictures of it last time, and it might be fun to take pictures of it in the snow."

Arnie did great leaps in the snow and so did Elliot. When they got to where the house was, there was nothing but a big bulldozer hovering over a pile of old boards. "The house is gone!" said Arnie, disappointed.

"Wow!" exclaimed Elliot, unable to believe what he was seeing. A sign with a giant high-rise apartment building painted on it had been put up. The sign read: Soon to be erected— Fairview Apartments.

"It sure was a nice old house," said Arnie, feeling a little sad.

"Yeh, but it smelled inside."

"That's because nobody took care of it." Arnie walked around the rubble. "I wonder what happened to the beggar and the dog."

"They probably moved to another old house," said Elliot.

"It's too bad they don't make houses like that anymore," Arnie said, looking up at the sky through a piece of pink-colored glass.

"Come out of there now!" shouted Arnie's mother.

He stood on the toilet bowl seat and looked

out of the narrow bathroom window. He counted the garbage cans in the alley, and watched an old gray tomcat disappear into one of the cans. "Happy hunting," said Arnie.

He was afraid to leave the bathroom now, because when he'd gotten home that afternoon he had seen the box of handkerchiefs on the kitchen table.

"Do you hear me?" continued his mother, turning the doorknob.

The cat jumped out of the garbage can carrying something in its mouth. "Have a good supper," said Arnie to the cat. Then he began to wonder if cats ate breakfast, lunch, and supper.

"Wait until your father comes home!" his mother threatened.

"But I'm on the toilet," said Arnie, truthfully.

"Don't give me that toilet business!"

"I really am," pleaded Arnie.

"You're just not normal," said his mother. "I don't know what to do with you. Maybe if you joined the Boy Scouts it would help."

The thought of joining the Boy Scouts made Arnie sick. He didn't want to learn how to tie knots or make a fire without matches or wear a dumb green uniform. But most of all, he didn't want anyone else telling him what to do.

"What do you think, money grows on trees?" shouted his mother. "I know what you did with that box of handerchiefs."

"It's not true," said Arnie.

"You didn't purposely throw it in a garbage pail?"

"I lost it," said Arnie.

"Don't you lie to me! I got my information from a very reliable source."

"Who?" asked Arnie, knowing very well who it was.

"Never mind who!"

"Who?" demanded Arnie, prolonging his stay in the bathroom.

"It doesn't matter. Let's say a little birdie told me."

"A fat little birdie with braces?" asked Arnie, clenching his fists.

"Gloria Becker happens to be a very nice little girl! But that's beside the point. Now you listen to me—" said his mother, her voice shaking. "Arnold, what makes you do these things?"

18.   Store for Rent

"How is your production cabinet coming?"

"It's not finished yet," said Arnie, who was happy to be sitting next to his father on the bus. It had been a long time since Arnie had spent a Saturday with him.

"If you really want something to get done, you mustn't put it off," said his father. Sometimes when his father spoke, Arnie felt as if he were also speaking to himself.

They had planned that day to go to an art museum and then to a surprise place, one that Arnie had to promise he wouldn't tell his mother about.

In the museum his father spent a long time in front of everything. "Isn't this something," he said. "All these things made hundreds of years ago are still around today for us to see and enjoy."

Arnie liked things from long ago also because he thought there was something mysterious about them. "I can't wait until I'm a great magician," he said, wanting his father's attention.

"It takes time and hard work to be great, Arnie. This museum can teach you that." He turned and examined another painting.

As much as Arnie liked the museum, he wanted to get to the surprise place his father had told him about. But after they left the museum it was lunch time, and so they went to a restaurant first.

"Mmmm, this is good," said Arnie, biting into a large corned beef sandwich. Food always tasted better to him when he was eating out with his father.

"Yes, it is," said his father, "but not as good as home cooking."

Arnie knew his father thought his mother was the greatest cook in the whole world. Some nights after dinner his father would say, "Mrs. Schiffman, that was delicious. You run the best restaurant in town." And his mother would laugh and say, "I know you married me for my cooking."

During lunch, his father asked him how he was doing at Hebrew school. Arnie told him all about the new rabbi and how nice he was.

"Maybe Rabbi Bliesch will stay in Miami," said his father.

"I hope so," said Arnie. He was happy to hear his father say that. It was good to have him on his side.

The surprise turned out to be an empty store with a *For Rent* sign in the window.

"What do you think, Arnie?" Arnie looked at his father, not knowing what to say. "I've thought about going back into my own business again, and this is a perfect spot for an appliance shop. They're building new homes all over this area."

"And could I put on magic shows in the back?"

"Sure!"

"Why don't you want Mother to know?"

"Well, I don't know if the timing is right. I mean, just after her operation—and you know how your mother worries about money all the time."

Sometimes Arnie wondered why people got married. "It looks like a nice store," he said.

"I see this store every day, to and from work. It just seems to be waiting for me."

"Then take it, Daddy." It seemed funny to Arnie, telling his father what to do. The store was near the factory Arnie's father worked in, so he took him to see it. It was a long brown building with a wire fence around it, and at the entrance was a guard.

"Hello, Bill," said Arnie's father.

"Hello, Joe," said the guard, surprised to see him. "You just can't stay away from the place, even on Saturday," he joked.

"I thought I'd show my son where I worked."

Arnie shook hands with the guard.

"He's a fine-looking boy," said Bill.

"Just a chip off the old block," laughed Arnie's father.

"You going to work here like your father?" asked the guard.

Before Arnie had a chance to answer, his father said, "No sir, not him!"

That night Arnie worked hard on his production cabinet, and through closed doors he heard his mother and father arguing.

"But you had a business and it failed," he heard his mother say. Arnie felt bad for his father. He stopped working and pressed his hands close to his ears.

19. No More Banana Cake

"**M**y mother is going to have a baby," whispered Elliot.

Arnie watched the print in the developing tray materialize. "When?" he whispered.

"In the summer, I think," replied Elliot, still whispering. "I heard her say she's three months pregnant, and it's February now, so I guess sometime in August."

"How do you feel about it?" asked Arnie.

"I don't know—it might be fun to have a a little brother or a sister."

Whenever Arnie and Elliot worked in the darkroom developing pictures they always whispered to each other, as if they were working on some secret experiment.

"I don't think my mother can have any more kids after her operation," said Arnie. "I heard her telling my aunt once."

Elliot lifted the print out of the tray. "Hey, Arnie! You're a terrific photographer! This is a great picture of your shoes half buried in leaves."

Arnie laughed, but then he studied the photograph. "If I must say so myself, that's not bad."

"Not bad at all. I bet you can enter this in a photo contest," said Elliot.

"You really think so?" asked Arnie, excited by the idea.

"Sure. You should see some award-winning photos in the magazines. Like there's pictures of watering cans, and old rusty nails in fences, and things like that."

The door to Elliot's room flew open. It was his mother. "Arnold, your mother just called. She wants you home right away."

"You almost ruined everything!" shouted Elliot. "You're supposed to knock at a dark-room door first."

While Arnie put his coat on, he looked at his photograph.

"You'd better hurry, Arnie—it sounded important," Elliot's mother said.

Arnie ran home, and found his parents waiting for him with their coats on.

"We're going to Bubba's," said his father.

"We just got a call from Aunt Fran. Bubba is very sick," said his mother, looking pale.

Aunt Fran greeted them at the door, and

they could tell from her eyes that she had been crying, The door to Bubba's room was closed. "The doctor's in there now," she said.

Susan and Amy were on the porch pretending to play Monopoly.

"Hi, Arn," they said, looking very sad.

"Bubba's real sick," said Amy.

"Do you want to play Monopoly?" asked Susan.

"No," Arnie replied.

"Neither do we," said Susan. "But Mother said we should keep busy since we just can't do anything to help."

The doctor walked out of Bubba's room, leaving the door open, and he told the family that they could go in. Arnie hid behind his father, and his mother rushed to Bubba's bedside.

"Mama, you'll be all right," she said, taking Bubba's hand.

Bubba looked very small in the large bed. Arnie was almost afraid to look at her. A blue oxygen tank stood in a corner. Arnie looked at Bubba's false teeth in the glass, and he wanted to hide them because he felt embarrassed for his grandmother.

When Arnie's father went over to her,

Bubba opened her eyes and said softly, "Joe, hold my hand." He held her hand, and then she closed her eyes. He turned away, and tears dripped down his face.

"Doctor!" shouted Aunt Fran. The doctor returned to the room and felt Bubba's wrist and listened to her heart. Then he covered her face.

Arnie's mother and Aunt Fran held each other and cried. Arnie, Susan, and Amy went out to the porch, wiping their eyes and blowing their noses.

"We don't have a Bubba anymore," said Susan.

"I'm going to miss her," said Amy.

"No more banana cake," said Arnie.

After a while Susan and Amy went upstairs, leaving Arnie alone on the porch. The vines outside the window made whipping sounds and Arnie looked up at the winter sky. He thought about Bubba going back to meet all the people she left behind in the old country, and he imagined her flying across the sky with the dybbuk she spoke about.

Arnie looked at the shriveled vines. Bubba would never see the leaves again.

20. Roses Are Red, Violets Are . . .

The cold days were growing fewer, and finally that one spring day arrived that seemed to touch everything all at once. Arnie left his coat behind and wore a sweater to school.

Miss Noonan announced the date of graduation pictures, and there were cries of excitement in the class. Graduation had always been a faraway thing, but the announcement made it seem very real and close. Arnie got a happy feeling. Graduation meant a lot of things to him—summer vacation, Junior High School, and no more Miss Noonan. And he thought about his birthday, only two weeks away. The classroom windows were open and the room was filled with springtime smells. A gentle breeze stirred the yellow forsythia branches on the sill. He closed his eyes and breathed in deeply.

In the street the ice cream man rang his bell,

and kids chased each other playing tag. Arnie bounded up the front steps to the rabbi's. It took a long time for the door to open and when it did Rabbi Bliesch was standing there. He looked the same, and on the table was the bottle of brown cough medicine. The rabbi was pale, and Arnie figured if he had been in Miami Beach he must have spent the whole time in a cellar.

Today the bench seemed harder, and the rabbi's voice seemed hoarser than he had remembered it. Arnie sat and waited his turn. He thought about how he liked to listen to Rabbi Marks sing, and what a nice voice he had. He also thought about how Rabbi Marks' yarmulke was always falling off, like his did, and how they laughed about it. He wished the young rabbi was still there—but all the same he was glad Rabbi Bliesch was okay.

The lessons were interrupted when the rabbi got up to search for something to blow his nose in. He returned from the bathroom with a roll of toilet paper. Arnie struggled through the lesson, and when it was over he mumbled, "Thank God!"

The rabbi looked at him sternly.

"Hey, Arnie! You won!" shouted Elliot from the window. "Wait! I'll be right down."

Arnie wondered what he was talking about. Elliot ran to Arnie holding a letter, and grabbed him around.

"You won fourth prize in the photo contest!"

"What did I win?" shouted Arnie.

"I don't know—fourth prize, that's what you won," said Elliot, suddenly looking confused.

"But I never entered any contest," said Arnie.

"Yeh, but I did it for you," said Elliot. "Fyfe Bros. announced a photo contest in their camera department, so I entered the photograph you took of your shoes."

"That's funny," said Arnie.

"The picture is going be on display at the store," said Elliot.

Arnie told his mother and father about the contest, and they both said they were proud of him. "We'll all go down to look at it," said his father.

At the store, Arnie felt good seeing his name under his photograph. Fourth prize was just a chance to enter another contest. But while they were in the store, Arnie's father bought him a small camera.

"Maybe I can be a magician photographer," he said excitedly.

"Maybe," laughed his father. "Maybe."

"Okay, everybody, smile!" said the photographer, hiding under a black cloth behind his camera.

The sun shone brightly in the schoolyard as Class 6-1 posed for their graduation picture. Arnie stood next to Robert Berry, who tickled him when the photographer snapped the picture.

After the picture-taking, everyone went back to the classroom and ordered their autograph books. Miss Noonan set the dates of graduation rehearsals, and warned everyone about getting spring fever.

At home that night, Arnie celebrated his twelfth birthday.

"You're growing up fast," said his father.

"Happy birthday, dear," said his mother, kissing him. They gave him two gift-wrapped packages. "One is for your birthday, and one is sort of birthday-graduation," said his mother. In one package was a book on magic, and in the other was a wristwatch.

Arnie had never had a watch before, and he had never thought of owning one. To him, watches were for kids like Gordon Rosewell and Rita Nadel. He felt funny about getting presents, because he felt that whenever he got one he should give something back, especially an important present like a watch. He put the watch on, using the last hole in the band, and it was too big for his wrist. "I guess I'll have to get a little fatter," he said. Arnie's mother baked a cake, and after supper they sang "Happy Birthday" to him. He hugged and kissed his mother and father. "Thanks for everything," he said, pushing the watch up his arm, and thinking. If only Houdini were here, everything would be perfect.

The autograph books arrived, and Arnie flipped through the pastel-colored pages, putting markers where the white ones were. Everyone knew that you saved the white ones for teachers and best friends.

In the front of the book where you write in your favorites, Arnie wrote in Elliot's name for best friend. His favorite color was blue, but he left the favorite teacher space blank. He gave his parents white pages to sign. His father wrote in a neat handwriting:

> Whatever path you choose,
> know that I'll always be
> there to guide you.
> Wishing you all good things always,
> love,
>   Dad

Classes were often cut short by graduation rehearsals, and every chance the kids had they signed each other's books.

"Do you want me to sign your book?" asked Gloria, seeing Arnie in the hallway.

"No, thanks—it's just for friends," said Arnie. Gloria turned away, with a hurt look.

At Hebrew school, Rabbi Bliesch announced the closing date for summer. He also told them to practice their lessons every day so they wouldn't forget them.

And at home his parents began to talk about summer vacation. Arnie's father said that he had heard about a farm that took in boarders.

"Oh, let's go, please!" pleaded Arnie, excited by the idea of going to a farm.

"We'll think about it," said his mother.

Arnie wondered why, just once, his mother couldn't say "Okay!" instead of "We'll think about it" or "Let's wait a while." He forgot about his autograph book and graduation. They didn't seem nearly as important as going to the country. He tried in every way possible to convince his mother to go there.

One night, Arnie's father said that he had to decide on his vacation dates—they wanted to know at work. A long discussion between his parents took place. "It will be good for you and Arnie," he heard his father say.

Arnie listened with his fingers crossed. "Please, God, make her say yes, make her say yes—say yes, Mother, please."

Then he heard his father say, "Good! That's final. I'll make all the arrangements, and we'll go the last week in July and the first week in August."

Arnie ran to the turtle, and put his head inside the bowl. "Did you hear that? We're going away, we're going away, we're going away!"

21. Graduation

It was warm in the auditorium and Arnie's flannel pants itched.

The principal and all the teachers made speeches, and a girl from another class read an essay on safety. Then everyone sang songs for a long time, and finally they were called for their graduation certificates.

When his name was called Arnie felt his cheeks burn, and he walked to the stage with his eyes on the ground. He shook hands with Miss Rogers, the principal, who wished him luck, and then he took his seat again.

After graduation exercises, his mother and father took him for ice cream. His mother asked why he didn't look up when he went to the stage. Arnie didn't answer.

Late that night Arnie got out of bed and looked at the calendar. He counted the number of days until they would leave for the farm. Then he went back to bed happy, knowing that he had to see Miss Noonan only one more time—for report cards.

The next day Miss Noonan wore the rose corsage the class had given her for graduation, and she had a big envelope with the report cards inside. Long before graduation the kids had talked about who would be promoted to the Rapid Advance class at the Junior High School. They all knew that getting into that class meant hard work, but it also meant skipping half a year. Everyone wanted to get into the RA.

Miss Noonan called the class by name, and each kid that got into the RA let out a cry when he received his report card. Arnie didn't make it. Only two other kids besides him weren't promoted to the Rapid Advance class.

Miss Noonan made a long farewell speech. Arnie wanted to yell, "You're full of baloney!" out loud and run away. But he remained silent and felt ashamed when it came time to say good-bye to the kids. The bell rang. Shouts of "School's over!" went up from the class. Arnie ran out the back door.

It was a hot afternoon. Arnie took off his tie and stuffed it in his pocket. He went to the canal and sat by the silk mill, listening to the looms humming. Inside he could see spools of brightly colored thread turning, and people wiping the dampness from their heads and arms.

He thought about what his mother often said to him: "You're just not normal! Why aren't you like other children?" He threw a stick in the canal and watched it float until it got stuck in a lot of garbage.

"Maybe if he spent less time with that magic stuff, he'd be better off," said his mother. She was upset about his not making the RA. But he couldn't understand what his magic had to do with school.

"It's not the worst thing that could happen," said his father. Arnie knew he was really disappointed.

"If he continues like this he'll be a dropout before you know it," she said. The word dropout scared Arnie, and he thought of the people working at the mill. "I'm going to be a great magician," he told himself.

He thought about running away from home. He thought of the movies he'd seen where kids ran away and kindly old men with dogs named Shep found the kids and took

care of them. And then they'd walk arou㹊
mountains and hike all day. The more Arn.
thought about leaving home, the less appeaₗ
ing it seemed. He might wind up like the beg·
gar and his dog.

"You should have joined the Boy Scouts,"
said his mother. "I don't want you hanging
around the house until we go away. All you'll
do is get in my hair." Arnie pictured his
mother with great heaps of hair and him getting tangled up in it.

He thought about some of his mother's ex-
pressions that he'd heard over and over again.
"You'll drive me to an early grave," she'd say
to him, or "You need some sense knocked into
you."

His mother continued talking about how he
should occupy his time during the summer,
while he imagined himself driving her to an
early grave.

"Arnold, are you listening to me?" shouted
his mother.

"I won't get in your hair," said Arnie. "I
promise."

He went to say good-bye to Elliot, who was
leaving for camp.

"I don't want to go to camp," said Elliot un-

happily. "But my mother said that with the baby coming it would be best if I was away. Anyway she's all nervous about it, because the last time she had a baby it was me, and that was a long time ago."

"You're lucky," said Arnie. "I wish my mother was having a baby. Then maybe she'd let me alone."

"I'll write to you, Arnie, if you promise to answer."

"I promise."

"Well, I guess I'll see you at the end of the summer," said Elliot.

"Sure," said Arnie, who felt bad about saying good-bye to Elliot.

They said good-bye, and Arnie sat in front of his building counting the days on his fingers until he could go away.

The next day Arnie woke up to the sound of music on the radio and the strong smell of furniture polish. His sheets were damp and twisted. The night had been hot and uncomfortable.

He stared at his breakfast cereal and watched the pieces floating on the milk. He

listened as the man on the radio spoke about the hot spell. And he heard his mother say, "I can't wait until we get to the country."

Some kids in the street had turned on the fire hydrant to cool themselves. Arnie walked past the lot where the tough kids were playing ball. "Hey you, hey you!" they shouted as Arnie passed. Arnie wanted to run, but he didn't.

"Hey you!" said one of the boys, catching up to Arnie. He felt his heart racing, like when he was in for trouble.

"Hey, do you want to be outfielder?" asked the boy.

"No, I gotta go someplace," said Arnie, sighing with relief. The boy turned and went back to his friends.

Arnie laughed to himself and continued walking. He walked to where the haunted house had been. Work had begun on the new high-rise apartment building. Arnie watched the showers of sparks as the workmen riveted the steel beams. A workman on a high floor waved to him. He waved back. Arnie thought it looked like dangerous work and wondered if he would ever be that brave.

He began to spend mornings watching work

on the building, and in the afternoons he discovered the quiet cool of the library, where he'd look through animal and nature books. He came across a picture of a dog that looked like Houdini. He checked the book out of the library and looked at it for long periods of time.

One night his father came home from work carrying a brand-new suitcase. "For the country," he said. Arnie got really excited because now he knew for sure they were going. His mother began to talk about what they were going to take along.

"You'd think we were going for a year," laughed his father. "We'll only be gone for two weeks."

"Can I take my production cabinet?" asked Arnie.

"Sure," said his father.

"We'll see," said his mother.

"What will I do with my turtle?" asked Arnie.

"I'm sure Gloria will take care of it," said his mother.

Arnie didn't want to ask Gloria, but he didn't know what else to do. She went into a

long thing about apologies and friendship before she said, "All right." But she also said,
"Then you'll owe me a favor."

After things were packed in the suitcase,
Arnie's father helped Arnie wrap his production cabinet and magic tricks.

It had been decided that they would leave
for the country on a Friday evening when his
father got home from work. That day seemed
extra long, and when his father came home
at night Arnie greeted him excitedly. His
mother made a last-minute check of the apartment.

"Well, we're on our way," said his father
picking up the suitcase.

"Wait!" said Arnie, rushing into his room.
"I almost forgot my camera!"

22. *The Applemans' Farm*

"Erie Lackawanna, Erie Lackawanna." Arnie repeated the words he'd seen on the side of the train. The train hissed and moved out of the station. He said the words again, as if it were part of some magic ritual. The train went through a dark tunnel and when it came out, the sun was low in the sky. Arnie could see people gathering on rooftops to escape the heat.

As the train left the city behind, the sky grew black and Arnie settled back in his seat and thought about the farm.

"Heightstown!" shouted the conductor.

"We're here!" said Arnie's father, grabbing up their belongings.

They waited on the platform, and it wasn't too long before they were greeted by a ruddy-faced, friendly-looking man. "I'm Mr. Appleman," he said. "You must be the Schiffmans." Everyone shook hands. He apologized and told them his car had broken down that day, and he had to come in his pick-up truck. He asked Arnie's father if he minded sitting in the open back.

"Not at all," laughed Arnie's father.

"Can I sit in the back too?" asked Arnie. His mother protested, and wanted Arnie to sit in the cab with her. But Arnie's father said, "Don't worry." And Arnie got to ride in the back.

The truck smelled of fresh-cut grass, and Arnie snuggled close to his father as the truck wove its way along winding roads. Arnie breathed in the country smells, and the stars had never seemed so close before. His father pointed out the Big Dipper and the Little Dipper and the Milky Way, things Arnie had only seen pictures of.

When they arrived at the house Mrs. Appleman greeted them. She was a big, friendly-looking woman, and she asked Arnie if he wanted a glass of milk. "It's from our cows," she said.

"You have cows?" asked Arnie excitedly.

Mr. Appleman laughed. "Yes, we have cows, and chickens and a horse named Bill. And if you wake up real early you can help me feed the chicks."

"I'll be up early," said Arnie, gulping down the milk.

Mrs. Appleman showed them to a large cheerful room with flowered wallpaper.

"A brass bed!" said his mother. "I haven't slept in one of these since I was a little girl."

Arnie's bed was brass also, and the mattress seemed extra soft. He fell asleep listening to the crickets.

The rooster crowed and the summer morning on the farm began. Arnie heard the low mooing of cows and the clanging of their bells as they were let out to pasture. He got up with his father and they dressed quickly and went down for breakfast. His mother said she wanted to sleep a little more.

From the smells in the kitchen Arnie knew that Mrs. Appleman must have been awake a long time. "Blueberry muffins," she said, putting down a large basketful.

Arnie was hungry and everything tasted better than it ever had before. When breakfast was over, Arnie and his father went out to the barn.

"It's just like all the things we've read about

in the farm game," said Arnie. The lofts were filled with hay and swallows chirped noisily on high wooden beams.

"Good morning," said Mr. Appleman, who had entered the barn carrying a large pail. "How would you like to feed the chicks?" he asked, tearing open a large burlap sack and filling the pail with chicken feed.

Arnie went out to the chicken coop with Mr. Appleman, and his father said he wanted to go back and see how his mother was doing. The little yellow chicks ran around Arnie's feet when he entered the chicken coop. He had never seen so many little chicks before, and he wanted to hold them all.

Mr. Appleman showed him where to put the food and how much, and where to put the water. "Chicks get thirsty too," he said. After the chicks were fed Arnie went back to the barn with Mr. Appleman. Arnie asked dozens of questions about the farm, and if Mr. Appleman had ever seen any wild animals. Mr. Appleman answered his questions and told him about the animals he'd seen. And then he told Arnie about the big owl that lived in the barn.

"He's a beautiful old bird," said Mr. Appleman. "Aside from myself, I don't think anyone else has ever seen him." Arnie wished that he could see the owl.

There were only two other guests at the Applemans' farm. They were an older couple who introduced themselves at lunchtime.

"Your son is a born farmer," said Mr. Appleman to Arnie's mother and father. Arnie smiled proudly.

"Don't get under Mr. Appleman's feet," said his mother.

"Mr. Appleman said I can feed the chicks every morning," said Arnie. Arnie felt a happiness that he had experienced very few times before.

In the afternoon the farm was drowsy. The cows stayed under the shade trees and the barnyard chickens disappeared into cooler places. Arnie's mother napped, and his father rested in a hammock tied between two large hemlock trees. "This is the life," he said to Arnie, who was watching a bee on some clover. Soon his father was snoring quietly.

"Cold lemonade!" called Mrs. Appleman, standing on the porch holding a big pitcher. As she filled Arnie's glass for the second time, she said to him, "Mr. Appleman says you take to the farm like a duck to water."

"I just like animals, I guess," Arnie smiled.

At supper his mother told everyone about Arnie's magic, and they all said that one night he must entertain. In bed that night Arnie heard the hooting of an owl.

The next morning Arnie was up before anyone, except Mr. and Mrs. Appleman. He dressed quietly and went downstairs.

"It's the little farmer," said Mrs. Appleman affectionately.

They ate breakfast and he and Mr. Appleman were out before the sun broke through the early morning mist. He helped carry the feed and then he took care of the chicks by himself. He noticed a chick smaller than the others who stayed away from the rest, and didn't come running when it was time to eat. Arnie picked him up and called him Chicken Little. He pecked at some food in Arnie's hand. "Hey, if you want to grow up to be big and strong you'd better eat," said Arnie, stroking the little chick with his finger.

When feeding time was through, Arnie walked through the high grass to the apple orchard. He saw Bill, the old work horse, standing in the stream cooling his feet and drinking water. He looked up when he saw Arnie.

"Mind if I join you?" asked Arnie, who took off his shoes and socks and went into the stream. The mossy rocks felt good under his feet. A frog jumped in the water and disappeared, leaving only a trail of bubbles behind. Arnie sat in a soft patch of grass, using a fallen tree as a back rest. He looked across the meadow and up at the sky and wished every day of his life could be like this one.

One morning Arnie noticed that the other chicks were picking on Chicken Little. "Is that nice, picking on someone smaller than you?" he scolded the other chicks as he fed them.

Then he ran to the barn in hopes of seeing the owl. Arnie thought how special things always seemed to be invisible, or happen at night when everyone is sleeping. That night after dinner, with the sky as his backdrop,

Arnie entertained for everyone. His production cabinet was a great success. After he pulled out a dozen colored scarves and a bouquet of crepe paper flowers, he pulled out the rubber chicken.

"I hope that's not one of mine," said Mr. Appleman. Everyone laughed.

They all thought Arnie was just great. Then Mrs. Appleman served homemade ice cream and they sat on the porch and looked at the moon.

The next morning, when Arnie went to feed the chicks, Chicken Little was dead. The other chicks had killed it. Feeling very sad, he buried it, and marked the spot with a stone.

That afternoon Arnie and his father went out berry picking. They walked along a narrow dirt road, shaded on either side by tall elm trees, and Arnie told his father about Chicken Little.

"The strong chicks weed out the weak ones," said his father.

"It's not fair!" said Arnie.

"But that's the way it is—it's the law of nature." His father stopped to pick some raspberries. "He's probably better off," he said,

trying to comfort Arnie. "Here, taste this!" He handed Arnie a plump raspberry.

They picked berries until they got a lazy feeling. Then they sat by the stream and ate the raspberries. Arnie had never seen his father looking so content before.

His father looked at the stream, and a faraway expression came into his eyes. "I remember when I was a boy, my mother would serve heaps of raspberries with sour cream. I loved that. So did my brothers. One time they all grabbed at the bowl and finished the raspberries before I had a chance to get at them." He laughed, remembering the story. "Boy, was my mother mad at my brothers. But she said to me, 'Joe, you've got to grab too.'"

"What was your mother like?" asked Arnie.

His father threw a pebble into the stream and watched the ripples vanish before he answered. "Oh, my mother was a very pretty lady."

"Did she have blue eyes, and a dimple in her chin like you?" asked Arnie.

The faraway look returned to his father's eyes. "Yes, her eyes were blue and she did have a dimple."

"Then she must have been pretty, because you're the best-looking father in the whole world," said Arnie, pressing his finger on his father's chin.

Arnie's father laughed and tossed another pebble into the stream.

On the last day Arnie felt sad, and asked his father if they could stay longer. "There's always next year," his father answered.

Arnie took a picture of his father in the apple orchard. They walked through the high grass together, stopping every once in a while to look at a flower, or a beetle, or to listen to the sounds of the cowbells. Climbing on top of a low stone wall, Arnie looked around and breathed deeply. He wanted to remember everything for a long time. He watched as his father picked up a cornflower and held it to his nose. He knew his father wanted to remember also.

Early the next morning before leaving, Arnie went to say good-bye to the little chicks. "Try to be good to the little fellas," he said, throwing them some feed. And when he went into the barn to say good-bye to Bill, he saw the big owl fly high up into the hayloft. He ran back to the house where his parents were waiting for him.

"I saw him!" he shouted. "I saw the big barn owl!"

23. Home Again

For days after the return from the country, Arnie thought about nothing else but the Applemans' farm. He began to visit the library again, and this time he recognized some of the flowers and trees in the nature books. And when he went back to see the construction work on the apartment house, he knew that when he grew up he never wanted to live in one.

Arnie got his turtle back from Gloria, thanked her, and promised to take her to the movies.

Some nights Arnie's father came home from work feeling so tired he went straight to bed. His mother suggested a check-up at the doctor's, but his father said, "It's just the weather."

The city did seem hotter to Arnie than when they had left it. He walked past the lot where he'd first found Houdini, and he knew he would never see him again. He had given up asking his father to take him to see Houdini—there was always some excuse. Arnie was restless.

Toward the end of the summer they went to the beach, and his father said the fresh air and sun made him feel good again. But he still looked tired. One very hot day was broken by a thunderstorm, and as Arnie ran for shelter he saw the beggar again. "There must be another old house somewhere," said Arnie.

Elliot returned from camp and apologized for not writing. He told Arnie he had a baby sister and that they were going to move. "My folks bought a house in the suburbs," he said.

Arnie felt both sad and envious, but he said, "Hey, that's great! I mean, moving into a house. I'll sure miss you though."

"Oh, we'll get together," said Elliot. "I'll visit you and you can come and visit me."

Arnie asked about what was going to happen to the store, and Elliot told him his parents were selling it and were going to open up a bigger one in their new neighborhood. Arnie thought about the store his father had wanted. When he had asked him about it later, his father said, "It's a thing of the past."

"I learned to play tennis at camp," Elliot said. "I think I might be a tennis player when I grow up," he said, swinging an imaginary racket.

On the day Elliot moved, Arnie sat in front of his building and watched the moving men at work. Elliot saw him sitting there and ran over to him. "Hey, Arnie, remember this?" he asked, showing Arnie the photograph he had taken of Elliot making a monster face. "That was the day we went to the haunted house," he laughed. "I found it when we were packing."

"That's practically an apartment house now," said Arnie.

Elliot wasn't listening. "You can keep this picture," he said.

The moving van pulled away. Elliot, his mother and father, and his new baby sister got into their car. "I'll call you!" shouted Elliot, sticking his head out of the car window. Then they drove off.

Arnie looked up at Elliot's windows and he could tell no one lived there anymore.

"But it's too big," complained Arnie.

"The way you're growing, it won't be big for long," said his mother, running her hand along the back of the jacket.

Arnie was getting school clothes. He hated the idea of starting out at a new school again. He just wanted to return to the Applemans' farm and be left alone.

On the weekend before school began, Arnie took Gloria to the movies as he had promised. Afterward, he told her all about the farm. "That sounds nice," she said. "It sounds better than where we live." He was surprised to hear Gloria say that—he didn't think she would like farms.

They began to talk about school and Gloria said it was a rotten shame that Arnie didn't make the RA. "Everyone knows you're smart, Arnie."

"No, I'm not," said Arnie.

"Don't put yourself down," she said.

He didn't want to talk about school because it gave him a sick feeling. He changed the subject and began to talk about the movie they had just seen. When Arnie left Gloria, she said, "Good luck in Junior High."

Arnie arrived at his new class early. In Junior High school there was a homeroom teacher, and a different teacher for each subject. When he arrived, his homeroom teacher was already there. It was a man teacher, which surprised Arnie, because he had never had a man teacher before. Arnie didn't count Rabbi Bliesch as a teacher.

"Hello," he said to Arnie. "I'm Mr. Phelps. Just take any seat." Arnie took a seat in back of the room. "We don't bite in this school," laughed Mr. Phelps. Arnie moved up closer.

The kids seemed different in his new class—noisier, and some of the kids seemed tougher, even the girls. One of the boys was Peter Kraft, the toughest kid Arnie knew from his old school; he had been left back a few times. Arnie felt like he didn't belong there, and he didn't want to be there. Mr. Phelps spoke to the kids and told them he'd also be their English teacher.

During the change of periods Arnie saw some of the kids from his old class, and he felt funny when they said hello.

The day dragged as first days do, and at the three o'clock bell Arnie headed home. When he was halfway there he remembered Hebrew school.

Rabbi Bliesch greeted Arnie at the door wearing a new suit, but the familiar bottle of cough medicine was on the table.

Willie gave Arnie a big greeting. "Did you have a good summer?" he asked.

"Sha!" said the rabbi, and the lessons began.

24. RA

One day shortly after school started, Arnie's father asked him how he was doing.

"I really think I belong in the Rapid Advance class," said Arnie.

His father looked at him in surprise for a moment. "Is there anything I can do?" he asked.

"I don't think so," said Arnie.

The next day during classes Arnie was called down to the principal's office, and he was scared. When he got there he found his father sitting with the principal.

"Hello, Arnold," said the principal. "Your father's been telling me about you. He tells me that you think you should be in the Rapid Advance class. I've looked at your records— your IQ tests tell me that you should be in that class, but your grades in the other school weren't too good." Arnie felt his face turning red. "I'll tell you what, if you get all A's this marking period you'll be transferred to the Rapid Advance class. Is that a deal?"

"Yes," said Arnie. His father shook hands with the principal and thanked him.

For the next few weeks Arnie worked hard and paid attention in class. He liked Mr. Phelps and Mr. Phelps liked him. One afternoon he asked Arnie to stay after class. "Arnie, as much as I like having you in my class, you really belong in the RA," he said.

Arnie was happy Mr. Phelps was on his side.

The Jewish holidays were approaching and Arnie's mother was planning the big dinner on Yom Kippur eve. "You'll have to help me," she told him. Ever since her operation she complained that it was hard for her to carry things. "You'll have to do some shopping for me," she said. Even more than washing clothes in the basement, Arnie hated to shop for his mother.

When Arnie got home from school one day his mother had a big shopping list prepared. "Don't be ashamed to tell the man at the fish store that if it isn't fresh your mother will send it back."

Although it was a rainy day, the fish store was packed with ladies shouting their holiday orders. They were impatient and pushed their way ahead saying, "It's my turn next; I've got a pot on the stove."

How could so many ladies all have pots on the stove, Arnie wondered. And if it was so, why did they do a dumb thing like go shopping while something was cooking? Finally, the clerk gave Arnie his fish.

Juggling an umbrella in one hand and a big bag of fish in the other, Arnie found it hard to protect himself from the rain. The bag got too wet. It tore, and pieces of fish fell to the ground. They slipped through Arnie's hand as he tried to pick them up. He was angry and embarrassed as he struggled to gather the pieces. Unable to use the bag, Arnie turned the umbrella upside down and carried the fish home in it.

"Don't you do anything normal?" his mother scolded, as she hung the umbrella out on the clothes line. "Some gefilte fish we'll have *this* year!"

On Yom Kippur morning Arnie and his father woke up early in order to get to the synagogue at the start of services. His father didn't have any breakfast, because on Yom Kippur everyone past the age of thirteen was supposed to fast all day. As Arnie put the last spoonful of egg in his mouth he asked his father why Jewish people didn't eat on Yom Kippur. "It's a form of atonement," said his father.

Knowing that Yom Kippur services lasted a long time, Arnie packed a sandwich in his father's prayer shawl bag. He carried the blue velvet bag with the Star of David on it, as his father had done for his father.

The synagogue was hot and crowded and Arnie sat between his father and an old man who smelled of lilac cologne. As the services went on, a young boy fainted. "He's probably fasting for the first time," said Arnie's father.

Arnie slipped his sandwich out of the bag and when his father was busy praying, he ate it. His father smiled.

At one point in the services everyone got up, and with their right hands in a fist-like position, they tapped their chests. "What's that for?" asked Arnie.

"We are touching our hearts and asking God's forgiveness," whispered his father. "Today God writes down in his book those who shall live and those who shall die in the new year."

Arnie imagined God sitting at a high desk with an old quill pen writing on long sheets of paper. "Do you think he'll get to the S's to-day?" asked Arnie.

His father laughed. "I'm sure of it," he said.

The day of report cards arrived, and Arnie sat nervously waiting for his. When he heard his name called he closed his eyes and whis-pered, "Please, God."

Arnie had a straight A average.

The principal called him to his office once again and told him of his transfer to the RA. "Keep up the good work, Arnold," he said.

"I knew you could do it," said his father, signing his report card.

25. Kaddishel

Arnie was happy to rejoin his old classmates. He was even happy to see Gordon Rosewell again. And everyone was happy to see Arnie. He sat next to Harvey Bloom. "No notes," he whispered, "please."

His new teacher was Miss Martin, who was young and pretty, and she told Arnie it was nice to have him in class.

He continued doing well, and even Rabbi Bliesch said Arnie's singing had improved.

During gym class one day Arnie was told to change and report to the principal's office. He shivered as he changed his clothing. It was cold in the locker room, but he also felt scared. His shoelace broke and he reported to the principal's office with one shoe untied.

The principal greeted Arnie in a friendly way. "Hello, Arnold," he said. "Why don't you sit down." Arnie felt nervous, and he could almost hear his teeth chatter.

The principal took off his eyeglasses and

looked directly at Arnie. "Arnold, you're a bright boy," he began. He turned from Arnie and looked up. "And I know you're a brave boy." Arnie couldn't keep his teeth from chattering—he knew something was very wrong.

"Arnie, I met your father only once, but I knew he was proud of you. Don't let him down." The principal hesitated a moment before speaking again. "I have to take you home, Arnie—your father has died."

For one whole week after the funeral, according to custom, Arnie and his mother sat on small wooden benches and the men from the synagogue came to say the Kaddish. Arnie joined in.

When the benches were taken from the house and the men no longer came, Arnie would sometimes read what his father had written in his autograph book, or look at the photograph he had taken of his father.

"You'll see, Daddy—I'll work hard."